PROPERTY OF
HIGH POINT PUBLIC LIBRARY
HIGH POINT, NORTH CAROLIN

JB   Ohno A Uschan   c.1
Uschan, Michael V.
Apolo Anton Ohno

Apolo Anton Ohno

Other books in the People in the News series:

Maya Angelou
Tyra Banks
David Beckham
Beyoncé
Kobe Bryant
Sandra Bullock
Fidel Castro
Kelly Clarkson
Hillary Clinton
Miley Cyrus
Ellen Degeneres
Johnny Depp
Leonardo DiCaprio
Robert Downey Jr.
Hilary Duff
Zac Efron
Brett Favre
50 Cent
Jeff Gordon
Al Gore
Tony Hawk
Salma Hayek
LeBron James
Jay-Z
Derek Jeter
Steve Jobs
Dwayne Johnson
Angelina Jolie
Jonas Brothers
Kim Jong Il
Coretta Scott King
Ashton Kutcher

Lady Gaga
Spike Lee
George Lopez
Bernie Madoff
Tobey Maguire
Eli Manning
John McCain
Barack Obama
Michelle Obama
Danica Patrick
Nancy Pelosi
Tyler Perry
Michael Phelps
Queen Latifah
Daniel Radcliffe
Condoleezza Rice
Rihanna
Alex Rodriguez
Derrick Rose
J.K. Rowling
Shakira
Tupac Shakur
Will Smith
Gwen Stefani
Ben Stiller
Hilary Swank
Justin Timberlake
Usher
Denzel Washington
Serena Williams
Oprah Winfrey

Apolo Anton Ohno

By Michael V. Uschan

LUCENT BOOKS
A part of Gale, Cengage Learning

Detroit • New York • San Francisco • New Haven, Conn • Waterville, Maine • London

This book is dedicated to Winter Olympics fans Lauren and Brandon Woods

© 2011 Gale, Cengage Learning

ALL RIGHTS RESERVED. No part of this work covered by the copyright herein may be reproduced, transmitted, stored, or used in any form or by any means graphic, electronic, or mechanical, including but not limited to photocopying, recording, scanning, digitizing, taping, Web distribution, information networks, or information storage and retrieval systems, except as permitted under Section 107 or 108 of the 1976 United States Copyright Act, without the prior written permission of the publisher.

Every effort has been made to trace the owners of copyrighted material.

LIBRARY OF CONGRESS CATALOGING-IN-PUBLICATION DATA

Uschan, Michael V., 1948-
  Apolo Anton Ohno / by Michael V. Uschan.
    p. cm. -- (People in the news)
  Includes bibliographical references and index.
  ISBN 978-1-4205-0603-7 (hardcover)
  1. Ohno, Apolo Anton--Juvenile literature. 2. Speed skaters--United States--Biography--Juvenile literature. I. Title.
  GV850.O45U83 2011
  796.91'4092--dc22
  [B]
                                                                    2011003418

Lucent Books
27500 Drake Rd
Farmington Hills MI 48331

ISBN-13: 978-1-4205-0603-7
ISBN-10: 1-4205-0603-X

Printed in the United States of America
2 3 4 5 6 7 15 14 13 12 11

Printed by Bang Printing, Brainerd, MN, 2nd Ptg., 06/2011

Contents

Foreword	6
Introduction	8
A Genius on Ice	
Chapter 1	13
A Father and Son Alone	
Chapter 2	24
Ohno Becomes a Speed Skater	
Chapter 3	36
Ohno Decides to Pursue Greatness	
Chapter 4	48
The 2002 Winter Olympics	
Chapter 5	61
The 2006 Winter Olympics	
Chapter 6	74
The 2010 Winter Olympics	
Notes	88
Important Dates	95
For More Information	97
Index	99
Picture Credits	103
About the Author	104

Foreword

Fame and celebrity are alluring. People are drawn to those who walk in fame's spotlight, whether they are known for great accomplishments or for notorious deeds. The lives of the famous pique public interest and attract attention, perhaps because their experiences seem in some ways so different from, yet in other ways so similar to, our own.

Newspapers, magazines, and television regularly capitalize on this fascination with celebrity by running profiles of famous people. For example, television programs such as *Entertainment Tonight* devote all their programming to stories about entertainment and entertainers. Magazines such as *People* fill their pages with stories of the private lives of famous people. Even newspapers, newsmagazines, and television news frequently delve into the lives of well-known personalities. Despite the number of articles and programs, few provide more than a superficial glimpse at their subjects.

Lucent Books's People in the News series offers young readers a deeper look into the lives of today's newsmakers, the influences that shaped them, and the impact they have had in their fields of endeavor and on other people's lives. The subjects of the series hail from many disciplines and walks of life. They include authors, musicians, athletes, political leaders, entertainers, entrepreneurs, and others who have made a mark on modern life and who, in many cases, will continue to do so for years to come.

These biographies are more than factual chronicles. Each book emphasizes the contributions, accomplishments, or deeds that have brought fame or notoriety to the individual and shows how that person has influenced modern life. Authors portray their subjects in a realistic, unsentimental light. For example, Bill Gates—the cofounder and chief executive officer of the software giant Microsoft—has been instrumental in making personal computers the most vital tool of the modern age. Few dispute his business savvy, perseverance, or technical expertise, yet critics say he is ruthless in his dealings with competitors and driven more by his desire to maintain Microsoft's dominance in the computer industry than by an interest in furthering technology.

In these books, young readers will encounter inspiring stories about real people who achieved success despite enormous obstacles. Oprah Winfrey—the most-powerful, most-watched, and wealthiest woman on television today—spent the first six years of her life in the care of her grandparents while her unwed mother sought work and a better life elsewhere. Her adolescence was colored by pregnancy at age fourteen, rape, and sexual abuse.

In every People in the News book, the author documents and supports his or her work with an array of primary and secondary source quotations taken from diaries, letters, speeches, and interviews. All quotes are footnoted to show readers where biographers derived their information and to provide guidance for further research. The quotations enliven the text by giving readers eyewitness views of the life and accomplishments of each person discussed.

In addition, each book in the series includes photographs, an annotated bibliography, a time line, and a comprehensive index. For both the casual reader and the student researcher, the People in the News series offers insight into the lives of today's newsmakers—people who shape the way we live, work, and play in the modern age.

Introduction

A Genius on Ice

Eldrick Tont Woods, George Herman Ruth Jr., and Orenthal James Simpson are sports superstars, who are much better known by their flashy nicknames of Tiger, Babe, and O.J. than the ordinary, even awkward names they received at birth. But one of the most instantly recognizable athlete names, one that is more interesting than most nicknames, is that of Olympic champion speed skater Apolo Anton Ohno. His name is easy to remember, because it is both unusual and interesting. Ohno likes it so much that he always asks the news media to use his full name in stories about his athletic exploits. "I've gotten a lot of compliments on my name," Ohno says. "Actually, I love my name."[1] What Ohno does not like is that most people do not understand his name's true meaning.

When Ohno's speed-skating prowess made him famous in the late 1990s, many people mistakenly believed his first name was a variation of "Apollo," the name of a god in Greek mythology. There is a Greek connection to Ohno's name, however. When Ohno was born, his Japanese American father, Yuki Ohno, wanted to give his son a distinctive name. Yuki combined two Greek words to create his son's first name—*ap*, which in English means "steering away from," and *lo*, which translates as "look out, here he comes"—and connected them with *o*. For his son's middle name Yuki chose *Anton*, a Greek word that means "priceless."

Ohno's father was only trying to give his son an interesting name. But Yuki ended up choosing words that would one day reflect the qualities that would make Apolo dominant in his chosen sport. In short track speed skating, as many as six skaters race against each other in one race. To win races, Ohno has to steer

Apolo Anton Ohno wears the three medals he won at the 2010 Olympic Games, which brought his total Olympic medal count to eight and made him arguably the greatest speed skater ever.

away from trouble and plot a course that allows him to pass his competitors. Thus many of the skaters he has whizzed by on his way to victory have had to "look out" for the rapidly approaching skater; some may have even thought to themselves "Oh, no! Here comes Ohno!" And, as of the 2010 Winter Olympics, Ohno has

A Genius on Ice

won eight medals, the most ever by a short track speed skater. These achievements have been "priceless" in boosting the image of speed skating in the United States and in making Ohno world famous.

But Ohno did not become famous because of his unique name. His name is recognizable around the world due to his accomplishments.

The Greatest Ever

One of Ohno's childhood heroes was heavyweight boxing champion Muhammad Ali, who liked to boast to the world and his opponents that "I am the greatest."[2] Although Ohno has never taunted rival skaters by claiming he is the best or fastest, it did not take him long to prove that he is as talented on ice as his idol was in a boxing ring.

Ohno excelled in swimming and roller-skating as a youngster but did not begin ice-skating until he was twelve years old. Ohno had so much talent and adapted to the sport so quickly that in 1997, a little more than two years after he began skating, he won the U.S. Short Track Championships. The fourteen-year-old Ohno was the youngest athlete to win a U.S. speed skating title. His victory also meant that he began representing the United States in races around the world. In the 2002 Winter Olympics in Salt Lake City, Utah, the nineteen-year-old skater's fame grew after he won gold and silver medals. Four years later in the 2006 Winter Olympics in Turin, Italy, Ohno won a gold medal and two bronze medals, and in the 2010 Winter Olympics in Vancouver, British Columbia, Canada, he captured a silver and two more bronze medals, bringing his medal count to eight.

Many people consider Ohno the greatest skater ever, because he has won more Olympic medals than any other skater. Jae Su Chun, the U.S. short track speed skating coach believes that Ohno's brilliance from 2002 to 2010, both in the Olympics and in international events in non-Olympic years, is proof that "Apolo is the best in history. He has everything. He tries hard, he is focused,

Ohno speeds through a heat in the fifteen-hundred-meter event during the 2010 Winter Olympic Games. His intense focus on and off the ice has been key to his success.

and he works hard. He has skated at a high level for a very long time. Some skaters at times can look better than Apolo but [that does not last long.]" Chun then gestures with his hands, raising and lowering them, and says, "Some skaters are up here, then down here. Apolo is always up here. Apolo is at the top all the time."[3]

Another admirer is Shani Davis, a long track speed skater who won gold and silver medals at both the 2006 and 2010 Winter Olympics, becoming the first African American to medal in a winter sport. In long track speed skating, races are decided by time alone, while in short track several people skate at the same

A Genius on Ice **11**

time to get to the finish line in races that have been likened to auto racing. Davis believes Ohno's fierce desire to win is what gives him an edge over other skaters. He says, "[Ohno] doesn't like to lose. He hates it so much, he's willing to go out and do things that no one else is going to do. He's very passionate about the things he does."[4] Davis means that Ohno is willing to work harder than other skaters to perfect his technique and make his body strong enough and fast enough to win races. Davis also says that mentally, Ohno is one of the strongest people he has ever known, an attribute most people would say Davis shares with his fellow Olympic hero.

Ohno Loves Skating

Despite his victories, Ohno has also had failures, injuries, setbacks, and controversies regarding races. After achieving early success, Ohno was so confident of his prowess that he quit training hard before the 1998 Winter Olympics. When Ohno skated poorly and failed to win a spot on the U.S. team for the winter games, he was so depressed that he almost quit skating. Even after winning his first Olympic medals in 2002, Ohno had to fight through injuries, jealousy from skaters from other countries, and other problems.

Ohno says that what motivated him to keep skating through the tough times was his love for his sport. In his autobiography, *Zero Regrets*, he writes, "Though I'm too tough on myself sometimes, I really learn from my mistakes. I love to compete—every minute of it, from the disappointments to the successes."[5] Passion for their sport and the ability to correct mistakes are what enable athletes to become champions in any sport.

Chapter 1

A Father and Son Alone

When Apolo Anton Ohno won his first medal at the 2002 Winter Olympics in Salt Lake City, Utah, he told reporters he owed his success to Team Apolo. The team was a small one—just Ohno and his father, Yuki. They had been a close-knit team throughout Ohno's life, because Yuki was a single father, who raised his son alone almost from birth. Ohno credits his dad with helping him develop mental and physical qualities that helped him become a speed-skating champion. Thankful for the way his father raised him, Ohno says, "I have certain times that I have to myself, I'm on the plane or I'm in a hotel room and I think like, 'Wow!' [I am] very grateful—you know, that I was blessed to have such great dad." Although it was difficult to be a single parent, Yuki is also grateful for the circumstances that allowed him to forge such a deep bond with his son. Yuki claims, "It was a tremendous experience to be with your child since age one. And every segment of the steps [of his life] he has to go through, I was with him."[6]

Yuki's dedication to helping his son realize any dream he had, even that of becoming an Olympic champion, was in stark contrast to the relationship he had with his own father. Yuki left his home in Japan when he was eighteen years old, because he did not want to follow the life path his parents had planned for him.

Yuki Immigrates to America

Yuki's father, a vice president of a Tokyo university, wanted his son to have a college education and to become a professional, like a teacher, lawyer, or businessman. In Japan only students who earn the best grades are allowed to enter college. Students who do not go to college have limited career options, so most parents expect their children to work extremely hard on their studies. Yuki's teenage years were consumed with getting good grades to please his parents. He studied so much that he was only able to sleep five hours each night. Yuki says it was difficult for him to meet the educational standard his parents set for him. He explains, "They expected me to perform academically high. It's the system over there [in Japan]. You've got to go the right channel [in schooling] from junior high and high school. [That includes] tutoring, testing and entrance tests, but once you pass the entrance test for college, it doesn't matter who you are, you've got it made."[7]

Yuki, however, did not want to go to college and then into a conventional job—he wanted to see the world and to have some fun while he was still young. When Yuki graduated from high school in 1973, he visited the United States. His first stop was in Portland, Oregon, but he soon decided to go to Seattle, Washington. Yuki liked Seattle so much that he decided to live there even though leaving Japan disappointed his parents.

Because Yuki spoke little English, he could only get low-paying, unskilled jobs, such as a dishwasher, a janitor, and a newspaper deliveryman. To improve his economic situation, Yuki attended Central Seattle Community College and became a hairstylist. After he graduated, Yuki was so talented that he won a haircutting contest. Yuki then decided to go to London, England, and enroll in a school run by stylist Vidal Sassoon, who had pioneered a revolutionary way to style hair that involved blow-drying and shaping the cut. When Yuki returned to Seattle, the new techniques helped him become successful, and in 1980 he opened his own hair salon.

In the early 1980s, Yuki met Jerrie Lee, who is Caucasian. The couple started a relationship and eventually married. On May 22,

The city of Seattle, Washington, is where Yuki Ohno settled after leaving his native Japan for the United States.

1982, Apolo Anton Ohno was born in Federal Way, Washington, a suburb of Seattle. Before Apolo celebrated his first birthday, his mother abandoned the family, and Yuki and Jerrie Lee divorced. Apolo never knew her and never got to know her son by a previous marriage, a half brother ten years older than he is. Ohno says he never felt abandoned while growing up, because he never knew the woman who gave birth to him. In his book, *A Journey,* he writes, "My father and I never talk about her because I have no interest in knowing her. It doesn't upset me and I'm not angry. I simply don't miss her, because she isn't in my memory and it's hard to miss something you've never had."[8]

At the age of twenty-seven, Yuki was a single parent. He was alone in a country that was still new to him in many ways and without any family to help him with his son. Raising Apolo by himself was a struggle in many ways for the young Japanese immigrant.

Ohno Never Knew His Mother

Apolo Anton Ohno never knew his mother because she divorced his father, Yuki, when he was an infant. In his autobiography *Zero Regrets*, Ohno writes,

> I know almost nothing about my mother. This is what I know: Her name is Jerrie Lee. She was adopted. She was several years younger than my dad when I was born. They split up when I was an infant. That's pretty much it. Because I was so young when my parents separated, I have no memories whatsoever of my mother. Zero. Not of her holding me. Not of her being there with me. Not of her kissing me. Nothing. It's a void, an empty space [and] I have no real desire to know her. [My] dad and I have talked about my mom only in bits and pieces. The only reason I even know what I do is because of a quick conversation he and I had several years ago. I asked him, "What's my other half?" He said, "I don't really know. I know your mom was adopted—but beyond that, I really don't know much." I remember only a couple of photos of her, and those are pictures that were around when I was much younger. That's it. Those are my memories. It's not weird and it's not selfish to say that I don't feel I have been shortchanged. My dad—he did it all.

Apolo Anton Ohno. *Zero Regrets*. New York: Atria, 2010, pp. 11–12.

Yuki the Single Parent

Yuki admits that when his wife left him he was not sure if he could handle the responsibility of rearing a child alone: "I felt, gee, can I do this. You know? I wasn't—feeling confident at all. I was scared."[9] Yuki constantly worried about being a good parent, because he knew he had to be both father and mother to his son. Although Yuki did not know much about raising a child, he knew he did not want to act like his own father had. Yuki knew that his father loved him, but they never had a close relationship. When Yuki was five years old, for example, his father took him to a baseball game. Because he was so young at the time, Yuki did not understand the sport, and his dad remained silent throughout the game, never explaining what was happening. Yuki was determined to be more of a companion and friend to his own son. He wanted to communicate freely with Apolo, take an interest in what he was doing, and teach him everything he knew.

Yuki had to work long hours to support his son, usually six days a week, so he placed Apolo in a day-care center until he was old enough to go to school. Yuki would drop Apolo off at day care on his way to work and pick him up on his way home at night. Sometimes Yuki took Apolo to his hair salon, and the infant slept and played while he worked. Once Apolo started attending school, Yuki ensured that his son got a good education. When a teacher complained that Apolo was not paying attention in class during a French lesson, Yuki realized that his smart son was bored. So he enrolled Apolo in a different school, one he hoped would better meet his son's needs.

To make up for the time he missed with his son because he had to work, Yuki took Apolo camping or to Iron Springs Resort in Copalis, Washington, when he had time off. The resort is in an isolated area along the Pacific Ocean. Father and son slept in the resort's small wooden cabins, walked along the shoreline, swam when it was warm, rode bicycles, and hiked in nearby wilderness areas.

Yuki even used the car ride on such trips to tighten his bond with his son. Ohno says that his dad "believed that the time we spent driving in the car was important too. You can really get to know your kid by spending hours and hours on a long drive."[10] Ohno understands how hard it was for Yuki to work long hours and be a good father. He explains,

> The kind of environment I grew up around was just challenging itself because my father was working so much. A lot of the attention and focus he would place on me was

distracted. He had to work and supply for the family, so I was a kid who basically had a ton of energy, was running around like crazy and really had no direction.[11]

The physical energy and athletic ability that would one day enable Apolo to excel as a speed skater emerged at an early age. When Apolo was five, Yuki bought him a bicycle. Yuki proudly took the bike out of the trunk of his car to show it to Apolo. But before he could get the training wheels out of the trunk and attach them to the bike, Apolo jumped on the bike and started riding. Even though Apolo rode slowly and shakily, he never needed the training wheels to help him learn to ride his new bike.

As a single father, Yuki Ohno, right, worked long hours to provide for Apolo, left, while remaining committed to building a strong relationship with his son.

Famous Sports Dads

Yuki Ohno is not the only father who helped his child achieve stardom in sports. Archie Manning is a former National Football League star whose sons, Peyton and Eli, followed in his footsteps as quarterbacks. Peyton played for the Indianapolis Colts and Eli for the New York Giants and both guided their teams to Super Bowl victories. Earl Woods taught his son, Tiger, how to play golf while he was still an infant, and Tiger went on to become the greatest golfer in the history of that sport. Like Earl Woods, Richard Williams introduced his daughters, Serena and Venus, to tennis when they were youngsters. By the time they were teenagers, the Williams sisters were winning professional tennis tournaments and soon became two of the most dominant female players the sport had ever seen. Yuki Ohno is different than those other fathers of sports stars in that he has no background in the sport his child chose. But like all three of those other dads, Yuki saw potential in Apolo to star in the sport he chose, and he did everything he could to help his son fulfill his dream of winning a medal in the Winter Olympics.

Yuki once described his young son this way: "At [an early age] he had shown me his unusual talent, especially in his mind, to be very, very daring. He shows lots of athleticism."[12] Apolo also showed early signs of independence, and his willful ways sometimes got him into trouble.

Father and Son Clash

Ohno's favorite book as a child was the whimsical *Green Eggs and Ham* by Dr. Seuss. As an adult, Ohno admits he liked the book because he felt a kinship to a character in it, who obstinately refuses to eat green eggs and ham. He says, "Remember how Sam tries to talk that guy into eating green eggs and ham? I was like that guy. I can be really hardheaded."[13] Ohno's youthful stubbornness and fearlessness led him to climbing to the tops of jungle gyms and refusing commands from day-care teachers to come down. He accepted dares from other kids to do things like eat dirt. As Ohno grew older, that defiant, daring attitude also led him to clash with his father.

Ohno was often alone after school until his dad returned home from work. He cooked his own meals and became skilled at making burgers, spaghetti, and even lasagna. But Ohno also had opportunities to get into trouble by doing things he knew were wrong. For example, when Ohno was a youngster he had two friends over to visit, and the boys started a fire in the fireplace. Ohno forgot to open the fireplace flue and smoke filled the house. Even though Yuki had told Apolo never to use the fireplace, he did not punish him because he was happy his son was not hurt.

Yuki also found it difficult to raise Apolo because parents of his son's friends were more lenient with their children than he was with his son. Yuki once said, "At other kids' houses, it's relaxed, their parents are their servants, kids' fingers snap, there's the

As an adult, Ohno is very close to his father, Yuki, right, but he admits that as a teenager, he often gave his dad trouble by being rebellious and difficult.

The Olympics Inspires Many Skaters

Although speed skating is popular in Europe and several Asian countries, it is a sport that does not garner a lot of attention in the United States. Generally, the only major media coverage speed skating receives is every four years during the Winter Games. This coverage inspired Ohno and several other American athletes to take up the sport. Ohno became interested after watching the 1994 Winter Olympics. Chad Hedrick, an in-line skater who won many national championships, was inspired by watching the 2002 Winter Olympics. When Hedrick saw former in-line skater Derek Parra win a gold medal in 2002, he started speed skating because he wanted to win an Olympic medal (in-line skating is not an Olympic sport). In the 2006 games in Turin, Italy, Hedrick fulfilled his dream by winning gold, silver, and bronze medals. An even more amazing example of the power of the televised Olympics to inspire athletes is Honolulu, Hawaii, native Ryan Shimabukuro. He became so interested in speed skating by watching the Winter Olympics that he persuaded his family to move to Wisconsin while he was still in high school. He did that because he needed to train at the Pettit National Ice Center in Milwaukee, then the nation's only Olympic-size skating rink. Shimabukuro never joined an Olympic team as a skater, but his passion for the sport led him into coaching. He became a coach of the national speed skating team and guided skaters through the 2006 and 2010 Winter Olympics to become the first Hawaii native in the Winter Games.

Chad Hedrick, a former champion in-line skater, celebrates after winning a silver medal at the 2006 Winter Olympic Games.

food." Yuki said that Apolo was so jealous of the greater freedom that his friends had that he would sometimes ask his dad, "Why do I have to come home?"[14]

By the time Ohno was thirteen, he was hanging out with kids who were seventeen and eighteen years old. A few of his friends engaged in vandalism, such as writing graffiti, and some were members of gangs like the Crips and the Bloods. Ohno, however, shied away from such criminal activity. He attended parties with those friends, but his dad always picked him up at 11:30 P.M., which embarrassed him because he was always the first to have to leave. Like many teenagers, Ohno began to argue with his father about many things, from what time he had to come home to where he was allowed to go. Ohno admits, "I think there was probably a period of time where we would just fight a lot, just about anything. It was mostly instigated by me, for sure."[15]

Apolo the Athlete

Partly as a way to place Apolo in positive, controlled environments after school, Yuki started him in a swimming program when he was six years old. Apolo quickly learned the different swimming strokes and began entering competitions. Yuki also made Apolo join the Northwest Boys' Choir. Apolo had a three-octave voice and was a good singer, but he hated singing and happily quit the choir when his voice changed after he reached puberty.

At the age of seven, Apolo took up roller-skating, because "I loved speed, and right away I wanted to race."[16] His dad began taking him to a roller rink every Thursday night, using the activity as an opportunity for them to spend time together. Apolo first skated on quad skates, which had four wheels on each skate. He began entering races and finished second in his first one. Although Yuki was proud his son had done so well, Apolo was angry he had lost. Apolo hated losing, so he began practicing and was soon winning races. When Apolo was eleven, he got his first pair of in-line skates and was able to skate faster than ever.

Eager to help his son pursue his new passion, Yuki drove Apolo to in-line skating races as far away as Missouri in his old Volkswagen

Rabbit. Apolo's innate athleticism helped him win races in both swimming and skating. At the age of twelve, Apolo won a statewide title in the breaststroke, and he also became a national in-line skating champion and recordholder among competitors his age. While Apolo was competing in in-line skating, he got the nickname Chunky because of his stocky, muscular build and his voracious appetite for pizza and other high-calorie foods.

But in February 1994, Apolo fell in love with a new sport when he and his father watched the Winter Olympics on television. Apolo loved the speed and excitement of short track speed skating the first time he saw it. In his autobiography *Zero Regrets*, Ohno writes, "It was like nothing I had ever seen before. The track was short. The ice was slippery. The racers wore tight-fitting competition suits that made them look like superheroes."[17] When Apolo told his dad the sport looked interesting, Yuki told his son he should try it. Three weeks later, Apolo put on ice skates and began racing toward his future as an Olympic champion.

Skaters battle for position in a race during the 1994 Olympic Games in Lillehammer, Norway. Ohno watched the speed skating competition on television that year and decided to give it a try himself.

A Father and Son Alone 23

Chapter 2

Ohno Becomes a Speed Skater

Apolo Anton Ohno's journey to Olympic glory got off to a shaky start in March 1994 when he took to the ice for the first time. Three weeks after watching the Winter Olympics, Ohno and his friend Zachariah Foster went to a skating rink near Olympia, Washington. A champion in-line skater, Ohno probably believed his transition to ice-skating would be easy. But Vince Foster, Zachariah's father, said the future Olympian quickly discovered how hard it is to maintain balance on such a slick surface. He recalls, "The first time he was on the ice, he was on his butt most of the time. I was kind of worried they [the two boys] would break something [and] to see him then, you'd never think he'd be the next Dan Jansen."[18]

Jansen was the long track speed skater from West Allis, Wisconsin, who had won a gold medal in the five-hundred-meter race a month earlier. Unlike Jansen, who was born into a skating family and was on ice almost as soon as he could walk, Ohno was an eleven-year-old novice, who knew nothing about ice-skating. His ignorance was evident when Ohno tried to use his new skates at a rink near Eugene, Oregon, famed for short track skating. Ohno had become reasonably good at skating since his first wobbly attempts, But when he tried his new skates, he said he had trouble gliding at more than a snail's pace until "another skater finally told me that I had to sharpen my skates."[19] Ohno did not know that new skates have serrated edges that have to be filed down. Ohno had a lot to learn about the new sport he had chosen.

A Reluctant Junior Skater

In 1996, Apolo Anton Ohno began training in Lake Placid, New York, with US Speedskating's junior team. Patrick Wentland, who was his coach, admits that Ohno hated being there at first and seriously considered leaving. But despite Ohno's bad attitude, Wentland was still impressed with the fourteen-year-old skater. He recalls,

> My wife Lynn was assisting me in Lake Placid. We were very concerned because [Ohno] spent a lot of time on the phone talking to his friends back in Seattle and they were telling him to "get yourself kicked out and sent home so we can have some fun." But he was good at coming to me and saying you know, "I'm not sure what I want to do. I want to skate but I also want to go back home and be with my friends." I told him, "It's your decision but make it on your own." [Ohno] was extremely mature for his age. He'd seen a lot more, done a lot more than most kids his age. Physically he was stronger than most of the other kids. Mentally, he wasn't sold on being there.

Patrick Wentland. Telephone interview with the author. November 10, 2010.

Ohno Takes to the Ice

Ohno began ice-skating because in-line skating, a sport in which he was already winning races, is not an Olympic sport. Like many in-line skaters, he switched to ice to pursue his dream of winning an Olympic medal. Ohno initially tried both long track and short track speed skating and was successful at both. He eventually chose to concentrate on short track. He explains, "There's more speed. It's more fun to be in a pack. You have to find holes to pass other skaters."[20]

It would take a lot of hard work, time, and money for Ohno to become proficient at short track. Luckily Ohno's father once again dedicated himself to helping his son fulfill his new dream. Yuki drove Ohno to rinks in Eugene, Oregon, and then Vancouver, British Columbia, Canada, to compete in races. Speed skating is a more prominent sport in Canada, and Ohno was able to learn more by watching Canadian skaters.

During Ohno's competitive swimming years, his father had videotaped his meets so he could learn from his mistakes and

Just as he did when his son was first learning the sport, Yuki Ohno videotapes Apolo's performance during the Olympic trials in 2001.

26 Apolo Anton Ohno

study techniques other swimmers used. Yuki did the same thing with speed skating, and Ohno began to learn techniques that helped him skate faster. He also began to understand the strategy skaters used to win races, like how and when to pass other

Best Friends

One of Apolo Anton Ohno's best speed-skating friends is Shani Davis, who won a gold and silver medal in both the 2006 and 2010 Winter Olympics in long track events. Although the Chicago, Illinois, native has had his most success in long track, he also competed in short track. Ohno and Davis met in 1996 at a short track competition at the Pettit National Ice Center in Milwaukee, Wisconsin. Ohno was new to the sport and did not know any other skaters. Davis introduced himself, and they bonded immediately because they had a lot in common. Both were minorities—Davis is African American—in a sport in which most participants were white. And unlike many skaters from smaller cities, they were both from large urban areas. Davis explains,

Speed skater Shani Davis, one of Ohno's closest friends in the sport, has won numerous national and world titles and Olympic medals.

> The first time we met was . . . at the Pettit. We were skating in a junior short track qualifying competition. . . . No one was talking to him, he was by himself. He was new to the sport. And I went over to him and we became friends right away. . . . We were both from a big city. He liked rap music, I liked rap music. And we became close right away.

Shani Davis. Interview with the author. Pettit National Ice Center, Milwaukee, WI. December 29, 2010.

Ohno Becomes a Speed Skater

skaters without bumping or blocking them, which can result in disqualification. Participating in the sport is expensive. In just one year, Yuki spent two thousand dollars on equipment for his son that included skates, a helmet, and skin-tight suits that made his body more aerodynamic so he could skate faster. His father also paid for use of ice rinks for training, entrance fees for races, and transportation and lodging for competitive events.

In Ohno's first short track competition in Eugene, a girl beat him in his first three races. But after studying the way she skated, Ohno finally beat her in the final race. Gradually, his skating improved. In his book, *A Journey*, Ohno writes, "What I remember most was how smooth skating began to feel. Smooth and quiet."[21] Ohno became so good that in January 1996, less than two years after he began skating, he dared to compete in the U.S. Junior Speedskating World Championships.

Ohno placed fourth in the trials. His finish was amazing because he was only thirteen, while some skaters were as old as eighteen and had skated since they were small children. Ohno added to his growing fame as a speed-skating prodigy a few months later by winning a national age-group title for speed skating. That led John Monroe, an assistant coach for the U.S. national speed-skating team, to state that Ohno had the potential to be a great skater. He said, "One of the things you try to keep in mind when you see a juvenile [skater] is that the transition from being very good to world class is often one that very few people can make. From what I can see, he will continue to develop [but] if he wants to make an international impact he will need specialized training."[22]

Ohno soon received an offer to get that training for free. But when it came, the golden opportunity created the most serious clash that Ohno and his father had ever experienced.

Ohno Rebels

In the spring of 1996, Ohno was an eighth grader at Saghalie Junior High School in Federal Way, Washington, when US Speedskating coach Patrick Wentland invited Ohno to move to

Lake Placid, New York, and train with the U.S. junior national short track team. US Speedskating, the governing body of skating, saw so much promise in Ohno that it waived the age requirement of fifteen so he could join the team. It was a huge honor for a skater so young. Yuki also saw it as a way to get his son away from friends he feared would steer his son into trouble. Wentland explains, "[Ohno's] dad was trying to get him out of the lifestyle he was in Seattle."[23]

Ohno, however, rejected the offer, because he did not want to leave his friends. "I was really angry, I didn't want to go,"[24] he said. Ohno's refusal widened a rift that had grown between father and son during the last few years while Ohno did whatever he wanted, even if his father disapproved. That included dropping out of his school's honors program and hanging around with older teens, who drank, smoked, and got into trouble. Once, some friends picked up Ohno in a car they had stolen, something that scared even him when they told him what they had done. Yuki was sad because he was becoming estranged from his son and believed Apolo's life was headed in the wrong direction. As an adult, even Ohno admits, "I was getting in too much trouble back home, and it wasn't good."[25]

Yuki kept trying to persuade Apolo to go to Lake Placid. He believed the opportunity could help his son achieve great things and felt it would be good for his son to get away from some of his suspect friends and change his questionable lifestyle. "He went through a very dangerous period," Yuki said. "He doesn't know what's ahead in that life. That's when I have to force myself to move him."[26]

On June 29, Yuki packed his fourteen-year-old son's bags and forced him to go to Seattle-Tacoma International Airport for a flight to Lake Placid. Yuki left the airport confident his son would obey him and get on the plane. Ohno never did. Years later he recalled, "I had it all planned. Dad told me, 'I know what's best for you, you need to listen.' He comes from that Asian background; he's strict. But I'm fourteen, I don't want to do anything anybody says. So I had a friend pick me up. I was gone."[27]

Ohno hid out for five days, sneaking home several times to get fresh clothes while his father worked. Yuki learned his son was not in Lake Placid when Wentland called him. When Yuki found out where Apolo was staying, he went there to get him but Apolo refused to go home. Embarrassed, Yuki left alone. As an adult, Ohno admits he is ashamed of his refusal, because it hurt his dad.

The next day, Ohno went home, and father and son talked over the situation. Ohno agreed to go to Lake Placid, but only if he could quit after three months if he did not like it. On July 8, Yuki and Apolo flew together to Lake Placid. Several days later on the return trip to Washington, Yuki worried about how his son would handle the huge change in his life. He recalls, "When I left, you could imagine the uncertainty. I didn't know if it was going to work out or not."[28]

Lake Placid

At first, Ohno hated training with the junior national team. He had to get up at 7 A.M. six days a week and run for an hour, skate for two hours, and lift weights for two hours. When summer ended, he trained nearly as much while attending Lake Placid High School, which was located next to the team's training facility. An angry Ohno initially responded by shunning coaches and skaters alike. But he gradually became friends with skaters like his roommate, Donald Stewart, and began to enjoy training. He recalls, "I started to have fun. All I had to do was train and go to school. That was a blast."[29] It was fun because Ohno was learning to skate faster.

Ohno had never had a coach, and the new skating techniques he was learning helped him improve rapidly. The skater, who had always preferred fatty foods such as pizza, was also introduced to proper nutrition. When team doctors measured skaters for body fat percentage, Ohno's was 12 percent, almost twice the average of other skaters. Ohno realized then that if he wanted to be a great skater he had to get serious about being in top physical shape. He went to Wentland, who he admired, and asked him to "make me a machine. I want to be the best ever."[30] It was a turning point for the young skater. Wentland recalls, "He came into my office and said 'I've decided to stay and I want to be the best.' His demeanor changed instantly that day and he started giving 100 percent at all the workouts. To hear someone that young say they wanted to be the best showed how mature he was even then."[31]

Ohno's new dedication quickly helped him become one of the team's best skaters. In October he was chosen to participate in a junior exhibition in Lake Placid during a World Cup competition involving skaters from the United States and Canada. Three days before the event, Ohno fell hard while skating and slammed into the ice rink's retaining wall. Ohno's right leg and hip hurt so much that he had to be carried off the ice. Ohno competed despite the injury, and he won. His gritty performance showed Wentland, his dad, and the entire world that he was serious about becoming a great skater.

Two months later in December 1996, Ohno went to trials in Milwaukee, Wisconsin, to make the U.S. junior team that com-

Ohno glides across the Olympic rings at the 2006 games, one of many times he has represented his country in speed skating competitions. He found a new dedication to his training and the sport when he began training with the junior national team at the Olympic facility in Lake Placid in 1996.

petes internationally against skaters from other countries. Ohno finished third, and only the top two skaters make the team. It was a huge disappointment, but it only made him train harder. And when Wentland returned from traveling with the junior team, he gave Ohno a valuable tip. Wentland told him to relax going into turns instead of trying to muscle his way through them as he had in in-line skating, and the new technique helped him. Ohno explains, "There's a fine line in everything between going too hard and just feeling the flow. Suddenly I felt the flow."[32] Suddenly, Ohno was skating faster than ever.

Success and then Failure

In March 1997, Ohno's hard work and new understanding of skating helped him make history at the U.S. Short Track Championships in Walpole, Massachusetts. The title is decided on points compiled in four races: the five-hundred meter, the

The Olympic rings greet visitors at the U.S. Olympic Complex in Colorado Springs, Colorado, where Ohno began training after earning a spot on the national team with his championship win in 1997.

The Biggest Failure of His Life

In 1997, Apolo Anton Ohno took a long break from speed skating. Although Ohno believed he deserved it after months of hard training, it ruined his chance to make the U.S. team for the 1998 Winter Olympics. Ohno says that he only had himself to blame for the biggest failure of his life. In his autobiography, *Zero Regrets*, he writes,

> In 1997 I did not train from April until almost August. I went back to being the me I had been before I went off to Lake Placid. I went right back to doing the same things I had been doing and to hanging out with the same crew, except they were now a little bit older, a little bit badder, and doing things they shouldn't have been doing. I slept late. When I finally got up, midmorning, I'd call one of my buddies, go over to his house, and hang out. Maybe we'd go to the beach. Or to the mall. Or to someone else's house. At night there were barbecues or movies and, after, maybe a party. [U.S. national team coach Jeroen] Otter had told me to put in lots of miles on the bike while I was in Seattle. I didn't. I also did not run or lift [weights] or stretch or even skate, at least very much. I did eat a lot of junk food. I gained—oh, a conservative guess would be maybe 25 pounds.

Apolo Anton Ohno. *Zero Regrets*. New York: Atria, 2010. p. 82.

thousand meter, the fifteen-hundred meter, and the three-thousand meter. The teenage phenomenon outskated everyone to win. Finishing second was thirty-two-year-old Andy Gabel, who had won a silver medal in short track at the 1994 Olympics. The veteran skater was amazed at Ohno's performance. Gabel said, "You just don't win national championships when you're fourteen. I've never seen anybody like him at his age."[33]

Ohno was the youngest skater to ever win a national speed-skating title. He also won a spot on the U.S. national team that competed in World Cup events in races around the world. As a member of that team, he began training with the older skaters at the U.S. Olympic Training Center in Colorado Springs, Colorado.

Olympic Dream Shatters

Making the senior team was an honor, but it proved to be a disastrous move for the fourteen-year-old skating prodigy. Ohno felt isolated socially, because he was much younger than other skaters. In addition, Coach Jeroen Otter had never trained such a young skater and had trouble helping Ohno do his best. In the spring of 1997 when Ohno went to the ISU World Short Track Speed Skating Championships in Nagano, Japan, he was overwhelmed both by the travel experience and having to compete against the world's top skaters.

White Ring Stadium in Nagano, Japan, was the site of the short track speed skating competition for the 1998 Olympics, which Ohno missed after failing to make the team.

After nearly a year away from home, Ohno decided spend the summer in Seattle even though he knew the 1998 Olympics was only months away. Instead of trying to improve so he could make the U.S. Olympic team, Ohno spent time with his buddies, ate whatever he wanted, and had fun. As a result, when Ohno reported for team training in August, he was 25 pounds (11kg) heavier than the 155 pounds (70kg) he should have been carrying on his five-foot, eight-inch frame. Ohno was in such poor shape that his coach sent him home to work out on his own. Ohno had promised to ride bikes, lift weights, and do other exercises, but he goofed off again and was still out of shape when he returned to Colorado Springs that fall.

Ohno tried desperately to get in shape for the January trials to make the Olympic team, but he could not overcome months of inactivity and finished dead last among the sixteen skaters who competed in Lake Placid. It was a dismal performance for someone who months earlier had won the national short track title and had believed he was a lock to make the team.

Ohno Goes Home

Ohno's feeling of failure to make the Olympic team was so great that he told Wentland he wanted to quit skating. Wentland told him not to make a rash decision without thinking it over carefully. When Ohno boarded a plane to fly home to Seattle with his dad, he was not sure if he would ever skate again.

Chapter 3

Ohno Decides to Pursue Greatness

On the plane ride back to Seattle on January 18, 1998, Yuki Ohno thought deeply about what had happened to his son. Apolo was devastated by not qualifying for the Winter Olympics, and Yuki knew he was not sure if he wanted to continue skating. Yuki believed Apolo needed to make that decision by himself so he could totally commit himself to whatever he decided. Before they landed in Seattle, Yuki told Apolo he wanted him to go to Iron Springs, the resort where they had spent so many happy times together, and decide his future. He also told Apolo he should not continue skating unless he was willing to dedicate himself completely to his sport. Yuki recalls, "I had to tell him, 'You have to do this alone, all by yourself in the cottage in a very rainy, cold isolated area.' It's very hard for me to tell him, but, 'You have to take this path to come to the decision on your own.'"[34]

After the plane landed, Yuki took Apolo to a store to buy food and then home to get some equipment and his cat, Tigge. They then drove two-and-a-half hours to the resort in Copalis Beach, Washington. Yuki told Apolo he did not care what decision he made but warned him not to call him to come home until he had made a decision. Yuki then left the fifteen-year-old to contemplate his future all by himself.

Ohno Makes a Decision

It was raining heavily the next morning when Ohno woke up. Except for Tigge, Ohno was isolated from the world; he would have to hike down the road to a pay telephone just to call his dad. Ohno had a small television, a video recorder to watch skating tapes, a stationary exercise bike, a refrigerator stuffed with frozen dinners and other food, and his running and workout clothes. With nothing to do except exercise, Ohno began pedaling the bike. When the rain stopped, he would run outdoors, even though he was not sure if he cared about improving his physical condition.

Because there was nothing to distract him, Ohno thought endlessly about the problem facing him—whether to continue skating or give it up. On January 21, his third day at the cabin, he began a journal that he titled *Dialogue*. In one entry that first day, Ohno confessed that if he continued skating by participating in the upcoming world team trials, he wanted to be in top physical condition so he could be the best skater there. He wrote, "I am skating to WIN, not second, not third, but FIRST and only that. If my dad helps me and I keep faith in God, myself, and my dad, I think I can do it. If for some reason I can't do it, then I know at least one very important special thing. I gave something 110 percent."[35]

For nine days he worked out and thought about his future. At times Ohno became despondent about continuing skating and questioned whether it was worth the effort. It took a toll on his body, too, because he was pushing himself so hard, biking inside or running outside in cold, nasty weather. He worked out not once, but several times daily and watched skating tapes in between while resting from the brutal sessions. His mind and emotions also got an intense workout as he tried to figure out his future.

On the ninth day, Ohno was running along the rocky beach in heavy rain. Drained both physically and mentally, he sat down on a large boulder and asked himself again if it was worth it to continue skating. This is how Ohno describes one of the most important moments in his life:

It was my third workout of the day. I was running and it was just pouring outside and I had like a hole in my shoe or something, and I was getting a huge blister and I was just so tired, and tired of training, and stopped. I just realized that if I was really desired to keep speed skating, I'm going to keep running. And I got back up and I kept running.[36]

Ohno finished his run and then called his dad, telling him only "I'm ready."[37] On the way home, he told Yuki he wanted to continue skating and would work hard to be the best skater possible.

Choosing the Dream

In early 1998 Apolo Anton Ohno spent nine days alone in a cabin in Copalis, Washington, to contemplate his future. He decided that he loved speed skating so much that he was willing to make any sacrifice to continue skating. Ohno knew that he would need as much help from his father, his coaches, and other people as he could get to realize his dream of winning an Olympic medal. Having made his decision, Ohno called his dad to come pick him up. In his autobiography *Zero Regrets*, Ohno writes,

> On the car ride back home, I told him. "I want to try this," I said. "Are you willing," he asked, "to really put forth a true effort? From the bone?" I told my father: "I want to skate." With clarity of purpose, everything suddenly seemed different. I didn't just want to skate—I loved it. I realized, too, that while I had to want to buy into the training, the discipline, the self-sacrifice, I needed direction and guidance, too. You truly can't get there by yourself. I needed not only to truly and profoundly depend upon Dad for help but also to welcome those—coaches, trainers, others—who could help me along the way. "I'm in," Dad said.

Apolo Anton Ohno. *Zero Regrets*. New York: Atria, 2010. p. 72.

Gearing Up for Greatness

The next day, Ohno flew back to Lake Placid, New York, to train with junior skaters. He did that because skaters in Colorado Springs, Colorado, were getting ready to leave for the 1998 Winter Olympics in Nagano, Japan. With a renewed determination to be a great skater, Ohno worked out tirelessly, as often as three times a day, to make up for the months in which he had slacked off in his training, which was the main reason he had failed to make the Olympic team. Once, Ohno pushed himself so hard during a workout that he fainted while trying to walk back to his room.

Two months later in March, Ohno competed in Marquette, Michigan, at the U. S. National Short Track Championship open to both junior and senior skaters. The top five skaters in the competition would make the team to compete internationally in World Cup events. Ohno got the final spot as an alternate, which means he had only qualified to skate in a few races. His diminished role on the team upset him, but he skated hard when he did race and tried to learn as much as he could from watching the world's best skaters compete. When the World Cup season ended, Ohno headed home to Seattle instead of spending the summer in Colorado Springs. This time, however, he would continue his training.

Ohno and his dad set up a gym in the garage of their home that included a stationary bike he would ride endlessly while watching skating tapes to learn about race strategy. He also ran at the local high school track and with the help of his dad did dryland training, exercises that help skaters increase their strength, flexibility, and balance. He also showed his renewed dedication to skating by not contacting his friends; he knew that partying with them would hurt his goal of becoming a great skater. Ohno also devoted more time to finishing his high school education. He had begun taking classes a year earlier through Internet Academy, an online public school, funded by Washington state. It was the only way someone like him, who traveled a lot, could finish school.

When Ohno returned to Colorado Springs in August, fellow skaters and Coach Pat Wentland—now the senior team's coach—were amazed at his new attitude. Ohno had been working hard to strengthen his body, and now he also began working on his mind and spirit by meeting with Dave Creswell, a sports psychologist the team hired. Creswell, who became his good friend, went on long runs with Ohno and introduced him to badminton, a sport Ohno grew to love. Ohno began to trust Creswell, who introduced him to techniques that helped him control his thoughts and emotions to become a better competitor. Creswell instructed Ohno on how to visualize how he would skate and win races and to meditate to calm himself during stressful times. Creswell also taught Ohno breathing exercises that helped him perform better physically.

As his body and mind grew stronger, Ohno began winning races and edging toward his goal of being the world's best skater.

Skaters compete at the 1998 Winter Olympic Games. After failing to make the team that competed in Nagano, Japan, that year, Ohno stepped up his training regimen and demonstrated a new commitment to the sport.

40   Apolo Anton Ohno

Speed Skating Equipment

Short track speed skating can be a dangerous sport. When up to six skaters are speeding around a 111.2-meter oval at up to 35 miles per hour (56kmh), it is easy for them to fall from contact with their competitors or lose their balance. When that happens, skaters can hit the ice hard, slide, and then explosively hit protective padding on walls bordering the ice. Injuries include concussions, broken bones, and cuts from their own razor-sharp skates or those of competitors who fall with them. To prevent injury, skaters wear specialized safety equipment. Gloves protect the hands of skaters from blades, their own or those of other skaters. Hands come into close proximity with skates when skaters make turns at high speeds; as skaters lean into turns, they often touch the ice with their hands to maintain their balance. Some skaters wear goggles to protect their eyes from wind and ice chips. Every skater wears a plastic helmet like those of bicycle riders to protect their head from crashes with competitors, the ice, and retaining walls. Skaters can wear knee, shin, or neck guards to protect themselves from the blades of other skaters. Even the skating boots they wear are specialized. Skating boots are higher on the ankle than traditional skates and made of sturdier materials to help keep the foot and ankle stable while they make turns at high speeds. The skates are also personalized for comfort and safety by being built from foot molds taken from each skater.

Ohno and other skaters compete while wearing the many pieces of safety equipment called for by the speed and danger of their sport, including gloves, goggles, helmets, knee and shin guards, and specially designed skates.

Ohno Decides to Pursue Greatness **41**

A Rising Star

Ohno's hard work finally paid off in a November 1998 World Cup competition in Székesfehérvár, Hungary, that featured skaters like Olympic medalists Kim Dong-Sung of South Korea, Marc Gagnon of Canada, and Fabio Carta of Italy. Ohno finished third in the fifteen-hundred-meter race. The victory boosted his confidence, and he looked forward to skating the thousand meter, one of his best races.

The thousand-meter race featured Kim, who had won the gold medal at that distance at the 1998 Olympics in Nagano, and Carta, another strong skater. With several laps to go, Ohno zipped past two skaters to gain second place; one of the skaters he passed was Kim. Ohno put on a final burst of speed in the last turn to skate across the finish line first. At age sixteen, Ohno was the youngest skater to ever win a World Cup race. He recalls, "I screamed in joy. Pat [Wentland] screamed, too, while the other coaches from other nations looked dumbfounded [and were saying] *Who is this kid!*"[38]

The victory made Ohno swell with pride that he could beat the world's top skaters, and he realized his victory was due to many things—his dad's faith in him; his long, fatiguing workouts; the many hours he spent watching tapes of races to understand how and when to pass other skaters; and the psychological techniques Creswell taught him. The big win made Ohno all the more determined to continue working hard and to become even better.

In a January 1999 interview, Wentland talked enthusiastically about his prize skater's physical ability: "He's a very strong kid for his age, incredibly strong. And he's extremely coordinated. I don't think I've ever seen anybody as coordinated as he is." Wentland noted that the real key to Ohno's new success was his new dedication to his sport. He said, "Skating is pretty much his life now. His friends at home basically don't exist anymore, which is too bad. But this is his extended family."[39] Later that same month, Ohno proved that his coach's assessment of his abilities was right when he finished first in the thousand- and fifteen-hundred-meter races and won silver in the five-hundred-meter event to capture the overall title at the U.S. Junior Speedskating

World Championships in Montreal, Canada. Ohno had made history again by becoming the first U.S. skater to win a junior world title.

Skating with an Injury

After winning the prestigious junior world title Ohno went to St. Louis, Missouri, for the ISU World Short Track Speed Skating Championships, where he again won the thousand-meter race and made it to the finals of the five-hundred-meter race. But in the championship final, one of Ohno's skates hit one of the small, round blocks that outline the turns of the oval course skaters compete on. The collision with the block knocked Ohno off balance, and he fell hard, sliding into safety pads covering the walls surrounding the ice. Ohno managed to get up but finished the race last. Doctors who examined him told him he had bruised some bones in his back but could continue skating.

At the ISU World Short Track Speed Skating Championships on March 19 in Sofia, Bulgaria, Ohno placed second in the five-hundred-meter race despite an aching back and finished fourth overall in another fine showing in his comeback. For the rest of the year, Ohno continued to train hard and skate well even though his back hurt. In December, the seventeen-year-old skater won the overall title in a World Cup competition in Chang Chun, China, which made him the youngest skater to win an international race.

Ohno continued to train hard and compete despite his injury because, like many athletes, he believed it was worth enduring such pain to be a champion. He explains, "[The pain] was something I lived with as a short track skater—something all athletes are taught to ignore—and I was too young and inexperienced to understand that my back needed more attention than a bag of ice and a massage."[40]

Despite the injury, Ohno continued to hone his credentials as the world's best short track skater. In a February 2001 World Cup event in Austria, he won the fifteen-hundred-, five-hundred-, and three-thousand-meter races to establish himself as a serious

Ohno Decides to Pursue Greatness

medal contender for the 2002 Olympics in Salt Lake City, Utah, which was now just a year away. But in March at the ISU World Short Track Speed Skating Championships in Japan, he hurt his back again weight lifting, and he started having painful back spasms. He had such terrible back and leg pain that in May he reluctantly saw a doctor, who said he suffered from a tear in a back muscle and a bulging lower spinal disk. The doctor recommended eight weeks of rehabilitation to heal the injury.

Ohno cheers after winning the silver medal in the 500-meter event at the ISU World Short Track Speed Skating Championships in Sofia, Bulgaria, in March 1999.

A Mature Young Man

Going into the 2002 Winter Olympics in Salt Lake City, Utah, Apolo Anton Ohno was the subject of countless newspaper, magazine, and television stories. Many reporters who interviewed Ohno were impressed by his maturity and how he had handled problems in his life, from not having a mother to his dramatic comeback after his 1998 failure to make the Olympic team. Journalist Lynn Zinser interviewed Ohno in 2001 for an article in a Colorado newspaper. She writes,

Ohno ties his skates in preparation for competition at the 2002 Winter Olympic Games, during which he was the subject of many articles and interviews that noted his poise and maturity.

Ohno has learned a lot from his failures, as well as his successes. He has learned to love the hard work, the quiet, dedicated existence in Colorado Springs, far from the kind of excitement that ruled his younger years. "I'm definitely proud of my past, good and bad," Ohno said. "It's what has shaped me into what I am today." [Ohno] dreams of winning medals in Salt Lake City, but swears it isn't the most important thing. "I think life is just one long journey and I think a lot of people look toward the destination and the results more than the journey," he said. "For me, the journey is where I find my excitement. The training, the dieting, the lifestyle I'm living right now. That's what I look for." He is 19 years old.

Lynn Zinser. "A Long Road to Olympic Short-Track." *(Colorado Springs, CO) Gazette*, December 15, 2001.

Ohno Decides to Pursue Greatness

Having to refrain from skating for that long was a crushing blow to Ohno's hopes to skate in the 2002 Olympics because the Olympic trials would be held in December, which was just seven months away. But Ohno simply pushed aside his fears that he might miss another Olympics and threw himself into rehabilitation by doing recommended exercises and undergoing the required physical therapy to heal his back. In late August when Ohno finally got permission to resume training, he worked as hard as he could to get in shape. Although there was still some pain, he was bothered even more by fears his injury would ruin his medal chances in the coming games. But when Ohno competed for the first time in October in a World Cup race in Calgary, Canada, he showed the world he was still a medal threat as he won the thousand meter and finished second in the three thousand. Now all he had to do was qualify for the U.S. team.

The Olympic Trials

Ohno had one more scare before the Olympic trials. About two weeks before the trials, he was driving home from practice in Colorado Springs, Colorado, with teammate Shani Davis. Although Ohno was driving 10 miles per hour (16kmh) below the 45-miles-per-hour (72kmh) speed limit because of wet snow covering the highway, his Toyota 4Runner suddenly slid on black ice across three lanes of the road. The 4Runner then hit the median and rolled over several times. The vehicle came to a stop on its roof, and the two young skaters had to kick out the remains of the shattered windshield to escape from the demolished car. "Good thing we had strong legs,"[41] Ohno said years later. Miraculously, neither skater was injured.

Those same strong legs also propelled Ohno and Davis to spots on the Olympic squad. Four years after his humiliating failure to make the 1998 team, Ohno dominated the trials by winning the five-hundred- and fifteen-hundred-meter finals and finishing third in the thousand. His performance also earned him the 2001 U.S. short track championship because the trials doubled as the national championship. Although Ohno was proud of himself,

Ohno, bottom left, was among the men and women of the team that represented the United States at the 2002 Winter Olympic Games in Salt Lake City, Utah.

his teammates were just as ecstatic that he had resurrected his career. Rusty Smith, who made his second Olympic team, noted, "He had four years of hell he had to go through because he skated as bad as he did at the last Olympic trials."[42]

However, due to a lingering controversy over the qualifying trials, Ohno would have to wait a little longer before he could realize his dream of competing for an Olympic medal.

Chapter 4

The 2002 Winter Olympics

Apolo Anton Ohno won three of four races to dominate the qualifying trials for the 2002 Winter Olympics in Salt Lake City, Utah. But Shani Davis, his best friend in skating, struggled to earn a spot on the speed-skating team. In fact, Davis had to win the final thousand-meter event on December 22, 2001, to make the team, and he did, making history. Davis was the first African American to make the team. He told reporters, "I'm overwhelmed with joy right now. It's a dream come true."[43] That dream, however, quickly turned into a nightmare for both Davis and Ohno.

An Olympic Controversy

After the trials ended, skater Tommy O'Hare filed a lawsuit claiming Ohno and skater Rusty Smith had allowed Davis to win so he could be on the team. O'Hare, a member of the 1998 team, felt cheated because Davis's victory denied him the sixth spot on the Olympic squad. Smith, who also qualified for the Olympics, finished second in the race, and Ohno finished third. Ohno had been so dominant in the first three events that some people wondered if he had skated slowly so Davis could win. Ohno's postrace actions also raised questions about whether he helped Davis win—as Ohno crossed the finish line third, he pumped his fist as if in victory. He then skated over to Davis and hugged him, because he knew his friend had made the team.

Cheating is wrong in any sport but seems especially dishonorable in the Olympics, which brings nations together for friendly competition and is dedicated to the highest ideals of sportsmanship. Eric Flaim, a former Olympian in both long and short track speed skating, explains why the allegations were serious: "A place on the team always must be earned, not given, otherwise the achievement is diminished. An ideal of all Olympians, as stated in the Olympic Oath [that athletes take], is to give your best every time you compete."[44] Flaim's comments carried additional weight because he had been the color commentator when the race was televised.

Ohno admitted he had not tried to win the race, because his only goal had been to make the team. Because he had already accomplished that, Ohno decided to ease off in the final race to make sure he did not injure himself and jeopardize his chance to skate in the Olympics. Ohno said, "I definitely could've pushed harder. But there's a time and place for that. The Olympics is the time to give everything I have."[45] An investigation by U.S.

Shani Davis, Rusty Smith, and Ohno skate the thousand-meter race at Olympic trials in December 2001. Smith and Ohno were accused of purposely letting Davis win so that he would make the Olympic team.

The 2002 Winter Olympics **49**

Speedskating into the allegations dragged on for nearly a month. Instead of joyously anticipating his first Olympics, Ohno lived in fear officials would kick him off the team if they decided he and Smith had helped Davis win. Despite the added pressure of the difficult situation, Ohno did a good job of preparing for Salt Lake City. Short track coach Tony Goskowicz said, "He handled it amazingly well. But it was still a mess, we lost a lot of training time."[46]

On January 24, 2002, less than two weeks before the games started on February 4, officials ruled there was no evidence to support O'Hare's charges. A relieved Ohno admitted he was excited about skating in the Olympics, and he said, "I was given a gift to skate and this is something I love. This is something I was meant to do."[47] Many other people agreed with Ohno's assessment of his ability and predicted he would star in Salt Lake City.

Olympic Predictions

In late 2001 and early 2002, newspapers, magazines, and television stations unleashed a flood of stories on the upcoming games, most of which predicted Ohno would be one of the event's biggest stars. *Sports Illustrated* magazine featured Ohno on the cover of its special edition that previewed the upcoming Winter Olympics and predicted greatness at the games for Ohno: "Here comes 19-year-old Apolo Ohno, the name summing up divine talent and ungodly trouble. Here comes the next U.S. Olympic hero. [Now] comes Ohno, a diamond stud in his ear, a whiff of scandal in his wake. He is a serious contender for four Winter Olympic gold medals."[48]

There were many reasons that Ohno captivated the imagination of sports reporters and millions of sports fans. He had a unique, brash personality and along with Davis was one of the few nonwhite athletes competing in the games. Ohno also had a sense of style that made him seem hip by comparison to other athletes. In addition to a diamond stud, Ohno wore a bandanna under his crash helmet to hold back his long hair. He also stood out because of his soul patch, a small tuft of hair just under his lip that became his trademark. Ohno had begun wearing the patch without consulting his hairstylist dad, and Yuki Ohno made jokes about it when interviewed by reporters, saying, "That surprised me when I first saw it. I think he was too busy to go to the barber shop."[49] Ohno says the real reason for the soul patch was that it was the only place he could grow visible hair when he was younger.

Ohno's superior talent is probably the main reason he drew a lot of attention. He was so dominant in his sport that he was considered a medal contender in all four short track events—the five-hundred-, thousand-, and fifteen-hundred-meter races and the five-thousand-meter relay composed of five skaters from each country. Many sports reporters even began comparing Ohno to Eric Heiden of Madison, Wisconsin, who two decades earlier in Lake Placid gave perhaps the greatest performance by any athlete in a single Olympics. In five events, Heiden won five long track speed-skating gold medals. And in an exhibition of excellence that may never be duplicated, Heiden also set world records at each distance from five-hundred to ten-thousand meters.

Many people also believed a stellar performance by Ohno would bring needed interest to short track speed skating, which was not popular in the United States. Pat Wentland, Ohno's former coach, said bluntly, "It's a dying sport [in the United States]. If Apolo scores big in Salt Lake and comes across as the personality he is, we finally have a shot to get noticed."[50] Wentland knew Ohno had a chance not only to popularize his sport but also to become a national sports star. Tens of millions of Americans who normally did not care about speed skating would be interested because the 2002 Olympics was the first their nation had hosted since the 1980 games in Lake Placid, New York. And because the 2002 Olympics came just five months after the September 11, 2001, terrorist attacks in the United States, it gave Americans still healing from one of the nation's greatest tragedies another way to express love for their country.

Thus Ohno went into the games carrying not only the burden of trying to win a medal but also of trying to boost the level of interest in the sport he loved. Ohno would succeed wildly in accomplishing both objectives.

Short Track Speed Skating

Many people who watched the 2002 Winter Olympics marveled at how Apolo Anton Ohno won his two short track speed skating medals. He took the silver medal in the thousand-meter race by sliding across the finish line after he had been knocked down, and he was awarded the gold medal in the fifteen-hundred-meter race when another skater was disqualified. Unusual endings are not uncommon in short track. Almost anything can happen when up to six skaters at a time, all of them wanting to cross the finish line first, race around the tight turns of a 111.12-meter oval at speeds of up to 35 miles per hour (56kmh). Skaters cut in and out of lanes to pass competitors, block faster skaters, and bump or touch each other, any of which can result in nasty falls and injuries. According to US Speedskating, the sport's national governing body,

> Short track races are fast, exciting and full of strategy, with speeds exceeding 30 miles per hour. Skaters race in packs of four to six skaters and race against each other, rather than the clock. [The] fast pace, along with the opportunity for contact and occasional spills, make for some of the most exciting racing in the world. *Time* magazine described speed skating as "human NASCAR" because of the speed, strategy and skill involved in the sport.

US Speedskating. *US Speedskating 2009–2010 Media Guide.* Kearns, Utah: US Speedskating, 2009. p. 36.

Ohno Mania

In the opening ceremony of the Olympics on February 8, Ohno marched into the packed stadium with athletes from around the world, even though he was feeling sick because he had caught the flu. Just four days before his first qualifying race in the thousand-meter event, Ohno was feverish, throwing up, and wondering if he would be able to compete. To prevent anyone else from catching the flu, Olympic officials had Ohno move from the village compound where most athletes lived to a hotel in Salt Lake City. His father joined him and nursed him back to health.

On February 13, Ohno made his debut as an Olympic competitor. When Ohno stepped onto the ice, he was greeted, to his amazement, by raucous chants of "USA! USA!" and "Apolo! Apolo!" from a crowd of more than fifteen thousand people. There were also banners in the stands that said "Ohno—Oh yeah!" and "Mission Apolo," a take-off on the U.S. Apollo space program of the 1960s and early 1970s that landed the first man on the moon. Some fans even wore fake Apolo soul patches.

Ohno's first race was a preliminary heat in the thousand-meter race. To loud cheers from the supportive crowd, Ohno finished second to advance to the quarterfinal heat. Later that night Ohno helped the U.S. team win its opening heat in the five-thousand-meter relay event. With seven laps left, Ohno sped away from the Italian team to take the lead. And when Ohno cockily glided across the finish line in first place and on just one skate, the

Ohno, center, speeds through a heat in the thousand-meter event during the 2002 Winter Olympic Games.

stands erupted in applause and cheers. Afterward, Ohno admitted he was almost as excited as the thousands of people who had cheered for him: "My heart rate definitely went up. This is the opportunity of a lifetime."[51]

It was a dramatic debut for the Olympic rookie. But just three days later, Ohno would be involved in one of the strangest finishes to any Olympic speed-skating race.

A Silver Medal

Ohno was favored to win the gold medal in the thousand-meter race on February 16 because two of his top competitors—South Korean Kim Dong-Sung and Canadian Marc Gagnon—had been knocked out in preliminary heats. The early leader in the five-skater championship final was South Korean Ahn Hyun-Soo. That did not bother Ohno, whose race strategy was to stay close to the leader and sprint to the front near the end of the race. With two laps to go, Ohno put on a burst of speed and darted by Ahn into first place.

As Ohno rounded the final turn with the lead and headed for the finish line, he seemed destined to capture the gold medal. But with just twenty meters to go, disaster struck. Li Jiajun of China tried to pass Ohno, bumping both Ohno and Ahn. Li and Ahn both fell, with Ahn's fall also wiping out Ohno and Mathieu Turcotte of Canada as his body slid into them. Ohno spun around 360 degrees before crashing back first into the padding surrounding the ice. Steve Bradbury of Australia, who had been trailing in fifth place, was the only skater left standing, and he glided across the finish line to win the race.

Even though Ohno had been knocked down, he knew the most important race of his life was not over—the second and third skaters who crossed the finish line that was just yards away would also get medals. Ohno tried to get up but was so dazed by the force of his crash that he fell down face first. The momentum of his fall, however, pushed him toward the finish line. Ohno kept on sliding over the icy surface and finally pushed his left skate forward over the finish line to win silver. Turcotte got the bronze with his own clumsy slide over the finish line.

Ohno was so excited about winning that he did not notice he was bleeding until he began walking off the ice. He had suffered a 6-inch (15cm) cut in his left thigh just above his knee from his own skate, something that can happen when skaters fall. He

Australian skater Steve Bradbury celebrates his surprise victory in the thousand-meter final after a crash among the race leaders allowed him to dash to a win. Ohno, on the ice, managed to scramble to the finish line to earn the silver medal.

needed six stitches to close the deep cut and to his surprise his doctor was Heiden, now an orthopedic surgeon. Ohno was then taken by wheelchair to the medal ceremony, where he hobbled onto the podium to receive his medal.

Ohno the Sportsman

Many people believe Apolo Anton Ohno was robbed of a gold medal by the freakish ending to the thousand-meter race at the 2002 Winter Olympics. But many people, including members of the news media, were also awed by Ohno's good sportsmanship in accepting what happened. In an article for the *Seattle Times* sportswriter Ron C. Judd writes,

> Ohno [was] a picture of class: Gracious, accepting, undeterred, satisfied. [When] he saw a gold medal he'd clearly earned stolen within sight of the finish line, Ohno could, legitimately, have cried foul. He could have called a press conference, summoned his attorneys, cursed the referees, berated the international federation and—as has become the custom of all too many Olympians—thrown a world-class hissy fit. Here is what he did instead: Hobbling on crutches from a 1.25-inch cut in the thigh he received in the pileup with Korean, Chinese and Canadian skaters, Ohno grinned, congratulated the stunningly fortunate gold medalist, Australia's Steven Bradbury, and said, "I skated the race of my life out there. I went off the ice happy." [Even] after a day had passed, Ohno had viewed the videotape, and the lost gold had a chance to sink in, the young skater [refrained] from constant baiting to launch another Olympic-officiating scandal. "It's not my place to say" whether referees should have taken further action, Ohno told NBC Sunday night. "I just went out there to race my heart out."

Ron C. Judd. "Gold-Medal Class Shown by Ohno." *Seattle Times*, February 17, 2002.

When the newly minted silver medalist talked to reporters a short time later, many expected Ohno to complain that Ahn's mistake had cost him a gold medal. But Ohno was satisfied with the result, because weird endings are part of his sport. He said, "This was the best race of my life. I skated it exactly like I wanted. Unfortunately I went down in the last corner. But this is the sport I train for. I got the silver medal, so I can't complain."[52]

Ohno vowed to continue skating despite the injury and then hobbled away on crutches, his left thigh swathed in heavy bandages.

Another Weird Race, Another Medal

Two days later, Ohno practiced for the fifteen-hundred-meter race that would be held in two more days. Ohno admitted to reporters that his injury still hurt but added, "I always feel pain. That is part of the sport."[53] His stoic comment referred to the minor aches and pains athletes in any sport ignore, so they can continue to compete. What Ohno did not tell reporters was that during practice he had skated so hard that the cut had opened and bled.

When Ohno took to the ice on February 20, fans waved American flags and greeted him with cheers, chants, and applause. The lusty reception was not only for his racing skill but also for his courage in competing with an injury. Ohno hung back from the lead through most of the thirteen-and-a-half lap race but with two laps to go made a daring move to pass three skaters and climb to second behind Kim Dong-Sung. On the next-to-last turn, Ohno sped up and dipped inside Kim to take the lead. Kim responded by moving into Ohno's path, forcing Ohno to straighten up and slow down, which allowed Kim to beat him to the finish line.

But when Ohno crossed the finish line right behind Kim, he pumped his arm in victory and smiled—he knew Kim had fouled him by blocking him and that judges would declare he was the winner. As Kim took a victory lap draped in a South Korean flag, Ohno calmly waited for a ruling by officials who were watching a video replay of the race to determine what had happened. When judges ruled Ohno had won the gold medal, the crowd let out

A Superstar

Apolo Anton Ohno was the most popular athlete of the 2002 Winter Olympics. According to a 2002 article in *USA Today*,

> To understand the all-encompassing impact Apolo Anton Ohno has had on these Winter Olympics, one needs only to look up into the seats of the Salt Lake Ice Center. Those stands are filled with fans who know even less about Ohno's chaotic sport of short-track speed-skating than they do about sumo wrestling yet arrive for events with patches on their chins, emulating Ohno's scraggly goatee. "Two years ago, I thought I was prepared. I thought I could handle 20,000 people, but it is totally impossible to prepare for a crowd that is that large and so supportive.... It was like I took in all their energy and excitement and put it into me [and] I felt like they were lifting me up.... When the announcer says my name and thousands of people start screaming the pain is gone, and I don't even think about it."

Ohno raises his arm to acknowledge the crowd during his gold medal ceremony at the 2002 Winter Olympic Games.

Tom Weir and Debbie Becker. "Popular Ohno Leaves Mark on '02 Games." *USA Today*, February 22, 2002.

A joyous Ohno proudly raises his gold medal after winning the fifteen-hundred-meter event at the 2002 Winter Olympic Games.

a deafening roar. Ohno hugged U.S. coaches sitting nearby and then went to the center of the rink, where he bent down and kissed the ice. Ohno was so ecstatic that he told reporters, "They can just throw me in the desert and bury me. I got a gold medal. I'm good now."[54]

"The Best Experience of My Life"

February 23 was the final night of short track competition. Ohno skated twice but failed to win a medal in either event. Ohno was disqualified in the semifinals of the five-hundred-meter race for blocking an opponent he was trying to pass. In the five-thousand-meter relay final, teammate Rusty Smith fell while skating, and the United States finished fourth, narrowly missing a bronze medal. The same type of strange happenings that had helped Ohno win two medals combined now to deny him two more. Because Ohno had been a contender for four medals, reporters asked him if he was disappointed he had only won two. He replied,

> It was definitely the best experience of my life—coming to the Olympics and performing so well. I'm definitely happy. I believe I did an excellent job. So many people supported me, all my friends and family and the fans, and that's just an unbelievable feeling. My first Games and I got two medals. There's nothing better than that.[55]

Chapter 5

The 2006 Winter Olympics

The 2002 Winter Olympics changed Apolo Anton Ohno's life by making him famous. He began to experience what that meant even before the games ended. After Ohno had won his silver medal, he and a friend slipped out of their room one night to buy food from a nearby delicatessen. As they were walking, Ohno's friend suddenly told him to start running. Ohno recalls, "I look behind me, and there's like forty people sprinting to catch up with us. I'm thinking: 'Oh my gosh. What have I done?'"[56] Those swarming fans eager to get close to the newly minted sports star were Ohno's scary introduction to being a celebrity. For the most part, however, Ohno enjoyed his new status as a sports hero.

Ohno the Celebrity

Ohno once claimed that "fame is a strange cat."[57] Up until the 2002 Winter Olympics, Ohno had been winning races and world titles in relative anonymity. Speed-skating competitions were rarely, if ever televised; the sport received little media coverage; and only small numbers of fans attended meets. But for two weeks the Olympics captured the world's attention, and Ohno and his trademark soul patch had become the most visible star. The nineteen-year-old was suddenly one of the world's most famous athletes.

When the Olympics ended, Ohno's celebrity life began with a round of television appearances. His first was on *The Tonight*

Show with Jay Leno. When Ohno got to the studio, he decided to shave so he would look presentable when he met Leno. But Ohno cut himself while using a cheap razor, and while he was trying to wipe away the blood, Leno came looking for him. Ohno recalls,

> I borrowed a razor in the greenroom [where celebrities wait to go onstage]—I had to use a cheap one with soap as shaving cream. I had a few nicks, and while cleaning up the mess, I heard that oh-so-recognizable voice: "Apolo? Where ya hiding at, buddy? What the hell are you doing?" It was Jay Leno. I felt like a knucklehead.[58]

When Ohno walked onstage, he was shocked that young women in the audience screamed his name as if he was a rock star. He appeared on other television shows, including MTV's *Total Request Live*, where he introduced videos and took questions from the audience. When Ohno showed off his break-dancing moves by doing a windmill turn on his shoulders and neck, the audience went wild. On the *Rosie O'Donnell Show*, the show's star handed an amazed Ohno the keys to a new car.

His home state of Washington declared March 14 to be Apolo Ohno Day. In a ceremony in Olympia, Washington, Governor Gary Locke told him, "We're so proud of you. You were amazing how you dealt with adversity. You truly embodied the Olympic spirit."[59] Locke was one of several state officials wearing fake soul patches to honor Ohno. After the ceremony, Ohno patiently and graciously signed autographs for hundreds of people, something he had grown accustomed to doing. When Ohno was in Los Angeles, California, in April, he had a chance to attend the Academy Awards ceremony. At the awards he met singer Elton John, a sports enthusiast who invited him to a party where he met stars like Harrison Ford and Halle Barry. He was stunned when many celebrities knew who he was and thanked him for representing the United States in the Olympics. Ohno felt strange mingling with so many famous people. He admitted, "I'm kicking it with the Backstreet Boys, asking them, 'So, um, do you guys play sports?' I don't think they even realize they're living in a different world."[60]

Ohno appears on **The Tonight Show with Jay Leno** *in February 2002 wearing his Olympic medals. His success in Salt Lake City earned him fame and media attention.*

To his amazement, Ohno discovered he was now a celebrity. *People* magazine named him one of its fifty most beautiful people for 2002 and *W* magazine flew him to the Dominican Republic and took pictures of him for its July issue. Former president Bill Clinton showed up for the photo shoot, and Ohno posed with him for a picture. *W* fashion director Joe Zee said Clinton and his daughter, Chelsea, "were in awe of Apolo, treating him like a celebrity."[61] Ohno modeled fashionable outfits for the photos, which he thought was funny because he rarely wore anything except workout clothes.

Ohno's fame soon faded as media attention shifted to other people and athletes making news. Ohno understood fame's cyclical nature. He said, "You don't disappear completely. Going on a plane, a couple of people might recognize me. But after the Olympics, there's only one way to go. Things have to level off."[62] That was fine with Ohno, who was ready to return to short track speed skating.

Another U.S. Championship

In February 2005, Apolo Anton Ohno dominated his teammates to capture his eighth straight win in the U.S. Short Track Speed Skating Championships. Ohno won all four races at the Pettit National Ice Center in Milwaukee, Wisconsin, but was not excited about his performance. That was because his goal was to beat every skater in the world in the same races at the 2006 Winter Olympics in Turin, Italy. When asked about his multiple victories, Ohno said

Ohno takes the lead in the thousand-meter finals at the U.S. Short Track Speed Skating Championship in February 2005. He won all four of his races.

"Winning isn't important. It's important to skate consistently the rest of the season. I've been consistent and I hope to keep skating well. My real goal is to skate even better in Turin."

Ohno used different tactics to win different races. In the five-hundred-meter race, he charged to the front and held the lead to the finish line. But in the fifteen-hundred-meter race, he had to charge all the way from fifth to beat Rusty Smith. Ohno is famous for hanging back until the final laps and then making a blistering move to the front to win. Even Ohno admits, "That can be dangerous, it doesn't always work out the way I want it to." Ohno said that was almost the case in his fifteen-hundred-meter victory: "The race was dangerous. Guys were passing all over the place. At first I kind of wanted to be up toward the front but then I decided to kind of hang back. It was a kind of a crazy race. It was tough."

Apolo Ohno. Interview with the author. February 27, 2005.

Apolo Anton Ohno

A Spartan Lifestyle

To the amazement of many people, Ohno moved back into the Olympic complex in Colorado Springs, Colorado, and began working his body mercilessly again to begin preparing for the next Winter Olympics. The complex is maintained by the U.S. Olympic Committee, which organizes and funds the nation's Olympic teams. The complex provides athletes in many sports with athletic facilities, trainers, and coaches to help them become better. Athletes can also live at the complex and even eat their meals in a cafeteria.

Ohno explained his spartan living situation to a reporter for *Rolling Stone* magazine: "It's rent-free, and they've got free food in the cafeteria. It's like dorm rooms. They're nice rooms, but I could use some more space."[63] Ohno's small room housed a big-screen television, a comfortable leather chair, and a small refrigerator filled with his favorite drink, strawberry-flavored NESQUIK. Ohno had to share his room and bathroom with Alex Izykowski, a young skater who admitted that "it was pretty cool"[64] to have an Olympic hero for a roommate. He said they enjoyed playing video games but that Ohno always won.

One reason Olympic athletes live at the Olympic complex is that, unlike professional athletes, they do not have much money. Professional sports stars can earn millions of dollars a year, but Olympic athletes get only a small stipend from the Olympic committee that pays for basic living expenses like rent. The amount is so small that most Olympic athletes have to work at least part-time to support themselves. Ohno was better off than many Olympic athletes because he had received thousands of dollars in bonuses for winning medals from the U. S. Olympic Committee. He also earned money from companies like Nike, Coca-Cola, and McDonald's, which paid him to be in commercials for their products, and for writing *A Journey: The Autobiography of Apolo Anton Ohno*, which was published in 2002. But Ohno had used much of that money to buy his dad a new home to reward him for the sacrifices he made to help him become a world-class speed skater. As Ohno told one reporter, "I'm not set for life, that's for sure. This ain't the NBA [National Basketball Association]."[65]

Ohno meant that speed skating was not the same as professional basketball, since professional basketball players make millions of dollars playing their sport. Ohno's one luxury was his truck, which he loved. He said, "Right now, I'm driving a black Toyota 4Runner. Sometimes I'll take a couple of hours and detail [clean] the whole car. I'll have it looking like a mirror."[66]

Except for trips home and vacations, Ohno's life revolved around training and competing in speed skating. He did not mind the sacrifices he was making because he loved his sport. In 2005 Ohno said, "I wanted to get back to what I do best, but it isn't because I'm a monk [who shuns fun]. It's cool to be the best and let people know you're the best."[67] The people he had to prove that to the most were South Koreans, who resented the success he enjoyed at their expense in Salt Lake City.

Ohno and South Korea

At the 2002 Olympics, Ohno won the gold medal in the fifteen-hundred-meter race because South Korea's Kim Dong-Sung was disqualified for interfering with Ohno. South Koreans were so angry at the decision that they flooded the U.S. Olympic Committee website that night with sixteen thousand e-mails, crashing its server. Some of the e-mails even threatened Ohno's life. South Korean animosity against Ohno was still strong in 2003. In fact, the entire U.S. team pulled out of a November World Cup meet in South Korea because of death threats against Ohno.

The hatred upset Ohno, who is part Asian and has many Korean American friends; he even liked singing karaoke in Korean. The anger against him gradually subsided and in October 2005 Ohno dared to compete in Seoul, Korea. Before leaving for Korea, Ohno admitted he was nervous about what could happen: "It only takes one crazy person to do something hurtful. That's what we're trying to avoid."[68]

Ohno was met at the airport in Korea by one hundred police officers in riot gear and received heavy protection wherever he went. He skated to victories in the thousand- and three-thousand-meter races and even drew cheers from South Korean fans who admired his prowess. The friendly reception delighted Ohno, who tried to win over the South Koreans by clapping for their skaters, signing

A South Korean man carries a sign expressing his disagreement with U.S. policy as well as his dislike of Ohno at a protest outside of the U.S. embassy in Seoul in March 2002.

The 2006 Winter Olympics **67**

autographs, and complimenting his hosts. According to U.S. assistant coach Jimmy Jang, himself a South Korean, Ohno ended the feud with his charming personality. Jang said, "He won them over by being Apolo. The anger [that South Koreans had about what happened at the 2002 games] was never really for him."[69]

Smoothing over the South Korea Situation

After the 2002 Winter Olympics, many South Koreans considered Apolo Anton Ohno a villain for having denied one of their skaters a gold medal. In an article in *Seoul Times*, a newspaper in South Korea, journalist Eric Gold discusses Ohno's reaction to the tense situation. He writes,

> "I was really bothered by it," Ohno said of the negativity. "I grew up around many Asian cultures, Korean one of them. A lot of my best friends were Korean growing up. I just didn't understand. Later on I realized that was built up by certain people and that was directed at me, negative energy from other things, not even resulting around the sport, but around politics, using me to stand on the pedestal as the anti-American sentiment." What made it even tougher to take is Ohno's father, Yuki, who raised him on his own, is Japanese-American. However, after the Olympics, the South Koreans seemed to have a better understanding of Ohno's position and were surprised by his dedication to the sport. This past October [2005] Ohno made a trip to Seoul for the World Cup [and South Koreans welcomed him]. . . . [Ohno said,] "I play no role [in politics]. I'm just competing. I was really happy with the crowd's reaction. Short track is very big in Korea."

Eric Gold. "Speedskating's Apolo Anton Ohno." *Seoul Times* (South Korea). Accessed October 2, 2010. http://theseoultimes.com/ST/?url=/ST/db/read.php?idx=2936.

Skaters from around the world at that time were already looking forward to the 2006 Winter Olympics in Turin, Italy. Ohno was once again expected to contend for more medals and in the months leading up to the games many stories mentioned the lingering animosity between Ohno and South Korean skaters and fans. But even Sung Jin Hyuk, a sportswriter for a Korean newspaper, said the skating feud was weakening. He even had a compliment for Ohno: "His lifestyle is just like Korean athletes. I think Ohno is a superb athlete."[70]

Sung meant that Ohno, like South Korean skaters, was so dedicated to his sport that he would do anything to improve. Ohno kept doing that because he burned with desire to win more Olympic medals.

The Turin Olympics

As the Turin Olympics neared, media attention focused again on Ohno. *Sports Illustrated* magazine featured him in its pre-Olympic coverage, claiming, "Ohno has become the marquee headliner of short-track speed skating, a sport that would otherwise get lost in the winter Olympic smorgasbord. But he revels in the attention he has earned [and] you can expect him to be in the spotlight again."[71] Ohno was even bolder when discussing his goals for the games, telling one magazine, "I want to be the best. I want to be the Michael Jordan of speed skating."[72] Jordan is considered to be one of the best players in the history of professional basketball. Ohno did not want to be just the best speed skater in the world but the best to ever lace up a pair of skates.

Ohno was entitled to make such brash statements, because he had dedicated himself since the last Olympics to becoming a faster, better skater. The athlete once nicknamed "Chunky" for his chubby physique had given up eating sweets and even his beloved pizza, because he knew eating healthier would make him stronger. Ohno weighed 165 pounds (75kg) in 2002, but four years later his new diet and his physical training had trimmed his body down to 157 pounds (71kg). To a vast, varied exercise regimen that included biking, dry-land exercises designed to strengthen skating muscles, and weight lifting, Ohno had also added martial arts training. He did that because he felt the martial arts would help him become a more fluid skater. All the hard work paid off as he won the overall World Cup title in the 2002–2003 season and again two years later. But South Korean Ahn Hyun-Soo had captured the crown in 2003–2004, and Ohno knew Ahn would be his biggest adversary in Turin.

Ohno's first race at the Turin Olympics was a disappointment. He was the defending champion in the fifteen-hundred meters, but he stumbled during a semifinal heat and failed to make the field for the final race. A despondent Ohno said, "I put a lot of dedication and time into this sport. To not even make that final and be able to challenge those top skaters, it hurts."[73] It hurt even more that Ahn won the gold medal, and Ahn's teammate Lee Ho Suk won the silver. Ohno made the final for the thousand-meter race, but the two Koreans once again finished first and second leaving Ohno with the third-place bronze medal. The finish frustrated Ohno, because he was trapped behind the two Koreans at the end of the race. He explains, "I was looking for a space to pass, but there was none. It's a tough position to be in."[74] Ahn swelled with pride and bragged about having beaten Ohno in two races.

Ohno stumbles behind Li Ye of China during the semifinal race of the fifteen-hundred-meter event at the 2006 Winter Olympic Games, a slip that took him out of the final race.

70 Apolo Anton Ohno

The Perfect Race

Apolo Anton Ohno claims he skated a perfect race to win the gold medal in the five-hundred-meter event in the 2006 Winter Olympics. He explains,

> The perfect race is different for everyone. It was perfect [because] I was able to lead from start till finish, which is very rare. And I just had total control over the race. I was completely immersed, I was in the zone, my flow was going, everything was going smoothly. When I got to the rink that day, it wasn't about trying to win. Obviously I wanted to win. But more, thinking back, I was really focused on the process of what it is going to take to be able to stand on top of the podium rather than I just want to win, I want to win. I was really concentrating on just skating. And I think that is why when I come across that line, you saw the look on my face. I didn't even know I looked like that. My helmet is tilted. I am like—you know, kind of freaking out because I really was almost in awe and disbelief. I mean that race is 40 seconds long, give or take a couple of seconds. But when I was out there, it felt like it was 40 minutes. Literally, everything slows down. And I have four guys behind me basically trying to eat me. So it was an amazing, amazing experience.

Quoted in Jaymie. "Olympian Speed Skater Apolo Anton Ohno." Asiance, January 31, 2010. http://www.asiancemagazine.com/2010/01/31/olympian-speed-skater-apolo-anton-ohno.

A Perfect Race

The five-hundred-meter race on February 25 was Ohno's last chance to prove he was a great skater. Ohno's semifinal heat matched him against lightning fast skaters like François-Louis Tremblay of Canada, the reigning Olympic champion at that distance, and Li Jiajun of China, a three-time world champion at five hundred meters. With two laps left, Ohno was trailing in fourth place, but in the last lap he managed to almost pull even with Jiajun for second place. The Chinese skater crossed the finish line inches ahead of Ohno but was disqualified for blocking another skater. Ohno advanced to the final and a chance to win a medal.

When officials start a race, they first call "Ready," and skaters then have to wait for an electric gun to be fired to begin. Individual skaters who start before the gun are charged with a false start, and if they have two false starts, they are disqualified. Canadian Éric Bédard was charged with a false start on the first attempt to begin the race, and at the second attempt to start the race, Ohno and

The five-thousand-meter relay team celebrates its bronze medal win to cap the 2006 Winter Olympic games. From left are Rusty Smith, Alex Izykowski, J. P. Kepka, and Ohno.

Tremblay had false starts. As the skaters once more lowered into racing crouches and awaited the gun, Ohno knew he could not afford another false start. But Ohno also knew he needed a great start to win the race. Ohno daringly anticipated the sound of the gun and shot off the starting line first. He raced to the lead and held it to win the gold medal with Tremblay second and Ahn third in one of the game's most exciting races. Ohno was ecstatic about his victory and declared, "I've been searching my entire career for the perfect race and that was it."[75]

Ohno topped off the night by leading the men's team to a bronze medal in the five-thousand-meter relay. Ohno was happier for his teammates—Alex Izykowski, J.P. Kepka, and Rusty Smith—than for himself, because they had never won medals. He explains, "The reason the relay is so special is because it's four guys fighting. Four guys with the same heart, the same passion. These guys can say they're Olympic medalists for life, and that's something special."[76] What Ohno did not say, but which reporters noted in their stories, was that Ohno now had five medals. That was just one less than the U.S. Winter Olympic record of six, held by long track speed skater Bonnie Blair. That meant the twenty-three-year-old skater had a chance in four more years to become the most decorated U.S. Winter Olympian ever.

Chapter 6

The 2010 Winter Olympics

After winning two medals in one night at the 2006 Winter Olympics, Apolo Anton Ohno told reporters the medals were worth the tremendous sacrifices he had made for years. He said, "The things you give up, this is the reason why. Everything goes into this. Days like this, you hope it lasts an eternity." But Ohno was growing weary of having his sport consume his life, and he admitted, "I'm 23 years old. I like to have a social life, and that's pretty much out the window [not possible for a speed skater]."[77] Since failing to make the 1998 Olympic team, Ohno had taken only short breaks from training and competing. After the 2006 Olympics, the twenty-three-year-old decided it was time to relax and do things he had never had time for in the previous eight years.

Opportunity Knocks

Ohno's post-Olympic life included sleeping late, easing up on the harsh physical regimen that made him a world-class skater, and eating foods he loved, like pizza. But he was still busy, because Ohno was now more famous and popular than ever. So many people wanted to honor and meet Ohno that he made a whirlwind series of public appearances. Some were fun, like tossing out the first pitch at a Seattle Mariners baseball game. But some were humbling, like meeting with soldiers wounded in the Iraq War. One soldier, Luke Murphy, told Ohno he was thrilled to meet an Olympic medalist. In his book *Zero Regrets* Ohno writes, "With due respect [to Murphy], the honor was mine."[78]

The Olympic hero also cashed in on his fame by endorsing products. Yuki Ohno said his son was not greedy, just an amateur athlete who needed to make money. "He's not like a professional athlete who has a multi-million-dollar contract with a team," his father said. "He has to have sponsorships to pay the bills."[79] Ohno became a spokesperson for nationally known companies, like Coca-Cola, Vicks, Omega, and Gap. Alaska Airlines even painted towering images of Ohno on several airplanes to boost its image with the flying public.

Ohno was interested in a career in entertainment, so he began spending time in Los Angeles. After the 2002 Olympics, Ohno played himself in the television movie *Skating Spectacular* and appeared on the *Hollywood Squares* game show. Ohno got an even bigger television opportunity when *Dancing with the Stars* asked him to be in its 2007 show. At first, Ohno was not sure if he should accept the offer. He could break dance but the show required competitors to perform ballroom dances with a professional partner. Ohno asked people he knew for advice on what to do. Fellow Olympic short track skater Allison Baver, whom he had dated for

Ohno autographs the side of a plane owned by Alaska Airlines, one of several companies with which he signed endorsement deals to capitalize upon his fame and success.

The 2010 Winter Olympics 75

several years, believed Ohno could do well on the show. She said, "He definitely has some moves. We've done some salsa dancing."[80] Ohno accepted the offer because of his fierce competitive nature—the show was another chance for him to win something.

But before the dancing began, Ohno had to do some more skating.

Ohno and Dating

Apolo Anton Ohno devoted so much time to skating from the age of thirteen until the 2010 Winter Olympics fifteen years later that he did not have much time for a social life. It was hard for Ohno to date because he traveled so much and because it was hard to find someone who understood his devotion to skating. Ohno began dating short track skater Allison Baver because being on the national team together made it easier for them to be a couple. However, skating got in the way of even their relationship. Turin, Italy, would have been a romantic place for a date on Valentine's Day in 2006, but Ohno and Baver were both competing in Olympic races the next day, so they did not go out. Baver was as serious as Ohno about skating. She quit dating Ohno before the 2010 Winter Olympics to concentrate on her skating, and in those games she won a bronze medal in the three-thousand-meter relay. In the following excerpt from a 2010 *People* magazine article, Ohno explains what appeals to him in a woman:

> "First and foremost," says Ohno, 28, "she has to have a good heart and good intentions. Those are key for me. A girl who appreciates trying new things is always great too." As for smokers, no thanks. "That's a hands-down deal-breaker." . . . "I haven't found my lucky lady yet. It's very difficult to dedicate all of my time to someone like that when my life is like this. It would be unfair for both of us."

Kate Hallett. "Apolo Ohno's Perfect Woman Doesn't Have to Skate." *People*, August 14, 2010. http://www.people.com/people/article/0,,20412907,00.html.

The Dance King

In February 2007 when Ohno entered the U.S. National Speed Skating Championships in Cleveland, Ohio, it was the first time he had skated competitively since the Olympics. When reporters asked about his long layoff, Ohno defended his sabbatical from his sport, saying, "It was well needed. I wouldn't say I'm 100 percent right now, but I feel pretty good."[81] Ohno was strong enough to win his eighth national title, because he had never completely given up his workouts and had prepared hard for the championship.

Ohno also skated in the 2007 ISU World Short Track Speed Skating Championships in Milan, Italy, from March 9 to March 11. In Italy, Ohno was both a skater and dancer because he had already started practicing for his appearance in the March 19 premiere of *Dancing with the Stars*. Julianne Hough, a beautiful eighteen-year-old professional dancer, was his partner, and she was teaching him how to dance. Hough even followed him to Milan to continue their lessons. Even though Ohno was sneaking out of his hotel room at night to dance, he won the fifteen-hundred-meter race and placed third in three other races.

Hough and Ohno practiced tirelessly for the show. But Ohno was so nervous before their debut dance, a cha-cha, that he panicked about his performance. In his book, *Zero Regrets*, he writes that before they began, he said to Hough: "I don't remember a single thing. What are we dancing to? I don't remember the music. I don't remember a thing." Ohno continues, "I never, ever had experienced this before a race. I had never blacked out. But this little dancing show—I was so nervous, so scared. I was dead-bang terrified."[82]

The cha-cha went well as did a fox trot, and Ohno and Hough tied for third in the judge's standings after the first night of competition. Other celebrity dancers included Laila Ali, daughter of Ohno's childhood hero Muhammad Ali; *NSYNC singer Joey Fatone; and former basketball star Clyde Drexler. Ohno's dancing soon began drawing rave reviews. After one memorable performance, judge Bruno Tonioli remarked, "He's pure entertainment. He should be a ride at Disneyland."[83] In the show's fifth week, Ohno and Hough's sexy samba scored the season's

Ohno dips Julianne Hough, the partner with whom he won the Dancing with the Stars *championship in May 2007.*

first perfect score of thirty—ten points from each of three judges. They matched that perfect score with a passionate paso doble in week ten.

The finale pitted Ohno and Hough against Fatone and Ali and their partners. For the finale, Ohno had his dad cut his hair, and many of his skating friends came to cheer him on. Ohno cut loose with some of his break-dancing moves in a freestyle dance that ended with Hough somersaulting over Ohno and landing on his

A Workout Fanatic

In the February 2010 article, "Winter Warriors" in *Men's Fitness* magazine, writer Nate Millado describes Apolo Anton Ohno's impressive workout schedule as he prepared for the upcoming 2010 Winter Olympics. Millado writes,

> Ohno's 12-hour training days include interval, high-speed, and endurance drills on the rink; "dry land" workouts on a track or bike; lifts and jumps at the gym; and post-workout ice baths. As the Olympics draw closer, Ohno is cutting back his workouts, but amping up the intensity. "It's not about how heavy you can squat or bench," he says. "I have to be as light as possible yet still strong enough to turn corners on one leg, on a blade that's 18 inches long and one millimeter thick." "If you want to build leg strength, jumping with resistance is probably the fastest way to do it," he says. Ohno does one-legged chest-to-knee jumps wearing a 45-pound vest, alternating explosive jumps on each leg with the raised foot behind him at 90 degrees and parallel to the floor. A simple yet effective exercise: walking sideways up a stairwell, one step at a time, bent low in a speed skater position. "This really builds your glutes, hamstrings, and calves," he says.

Nate Millado. "Winter Warriors." *Men's Fitness*, February 2010. p. 40.

shoulders. The audience went wild, and the judges again awarded them perfect marks. Ohno and Hough won the championship through points from judges and telephone votes from viewers. The night Ohno became a dance king was May 22, his twenty-fifth birthday. He said joyously, "This is perfect. This is definitely my best birthday ever!"[84]

Ohno clearly enjoyed participating in *Dancing with the Stars*. Now that it was over, he was uncertain whether to return to training for the 2010 Winter Olympics in Vancouver, British Columbia, Canada, or to pursue a career outside the sport he loved.

Returns to the Ice

One reason Ohno was not sure whether he wanted to continue skating is that his appearance on *Dancing with the Stars* had earned him fans who had never known him as a speed skater. His heightened fame could help Ohno start a career in entertainment or business, but he knew he had a narrow time frame before that new celebrity status would start to fade. On the other hand, competing in the 2010 Olympics would give him chance to surpass the six-medal total of long track speed skater Bonnie Blair, who was the most decorated U.S. winter athlete ever.

In the end, Ohno's decision was the same one he had made in 1998 while sitting on a rock in the rain after he had failed to qualify for the Winter Olympics—he still wanted to skate. Ohno explains,

> I know that I was meant to skate. Whether it's to stand on the podium again or deliver a different message, I don't know. I've won everything that I can possibly win [but] I really, honestly, in my heart believe there's a reason why I'm still skating. There's a reason I'm still healthy, a reason I'm still winning, a reason I'm still here.[85]

Once Ohno committed himself anew to his sport, he became willing to make any sacrifice to be the best skater possible.

Prepares for the Olympics

For several weeks in the summer of 2007, Ohno and Hough performed in various cities with other couples from *Dancing with the Stars*. When the tour ended, Ohno was out of shape for a speed skater and even had an improbable roll of fat around his waist. He then began working out harder than ever to prepare not only for the 2008 skating season but also for the 2010 Olympics which was less than two years away.

Ohno weighed 157 pounds (71kg) during the 2002 and 2006 Olympics but wanted to lose weight to skate faster in 2010. When Ohno skated in the Olympics in February 2010, he weighed 145 pounds (66kg) and had reduced his body fat to an infinitesimal 2.8 percent. The skater strengthened and streamlined his body through strict nutrition—he ate vegetables, fruit, fish, brown rice, and seaweed—and various punishing exercises. He lifted 1,000 pounds (454kg) with just one leg, hopped over benches on just one leg, and ran endlessly on treadmills or outside. And he worked out three times a day.

Although Ohno had bought a home in Salt Lake City, he also spent time at the Olympic training center in Colorado Springs, Colorado. His favorite workout there was the Incline, a trail made of railroad ties that snaked up Pike's Peak. The trail was about 1 mile (1.6km) long and rose 2,000 feet (610m) to an elevation of 8,500 feet (2,591m). Running it was the most tortuous way to get in shape Ohno had ever experienced. He said, "It's the one workout where people truly have to face something that is unbeatable. It is you against yourself."[86] Ohno endured it repeatedly, because he was willing to absorb any physical punishment to get in superb shape.

Jae Su Chun, a South Korean, became the short track team coach in 2007. Chun had coached many skaters but said of Ohno, "He's the [hardest] worker I've ever seen before, the most focused skater."[87] Chun and assistant coach Jimmy Jang both helped Ohno improve his skating technique and race strategy, such as when and how to alter his skating tempo during races. The results of his hard work paid off in 2008 when Ohno won the overall title at the world championships in March 2008 in Gangneung, South Korea.

Ohno struggled early in the 2009 World Cup season. He responded by increasing his already strenuous training program and began winning races again. By the time Ohno went to Vancouver in February 2010, he was confident he would win more medals. So was *Sports Illustrated* magazine. In its Olympic preview issue it predicted Ohno would surpass Blair's six medals because "as he proved in winning *Dancing With The Stars* in 2007, the man with the soul patch can handle the pressure."[88]

The Vancouver Olympics

The fifteen-hundred-meter race was Ohno's first. When Ohno skated onto the ice for the race, people cheered and held up banners saying, "Ohno Is Uno" and "It's Apolo's World. We're Just Visiting." Ohno, however, got off to a bad start and with a half lap left was out of medal contention as he trailed three South Koreans. But on the final turn when Lee Ho-Suk tried to pass leader Lee Jung-Su, Lee bumped him and both skaters fell. Ohno was not involved in the collision and glided to the silver medal He later told reporters, "No apologies. That's short track, man. Crazy stuff happens all the time."[89] Ohno made history by tying Blair for the most medals won by any U.S. Winter Olympian. He and teammate J.R. Celski also made history—when Celski came in third, it was the first time two U.S. short track skaters had won medals in the same race. Ohno threw Celski over his shoulder, draped an American flag over him, and skated a victory lap out of pure joy over their accomplishments.

The thousand-meter race was on February 20. Ohno grabbed the lead with just over two laps remaining and appeared headed for a gold medal until he stumbled and fell to last place. But Ohno charged hard after the mistake and passed Canadian brothers Charles and François Hamelin and won the bronze medal. Ohno then skated around the rink while holding aloft an American flag and seven fingers, the number of medals that now made him the most decorated U.S. Winter Olympian in history. Proudly watching was his father, Yuki, who told reporters, "He senses how important this is to his life and career. [His] deep-rooted passion for the Olympics and what that means have motivated him."[90]

Ohno holds up seven fingers, one for each of his Olympic medals, after winning bronze in the thousand-meter event at the 2010 Winter Olympics. He later went on to win one more medal in those games.

The 2010 Winter Olympics **83**

Helping Other Kids

Apolo Anton Ohno knows that if he had not had a supportive father and the talent to become an Olympic speed skater, he could have easily messed up his life when he was a teenager. It was his father's guidance and the lure of skating that drew him away from friends who were leading him into trouble. Ohno visits schools in the hope that his story can help teenagers in trouble to straighten out their own lives. Ohno explains why he feels so lucky to have the kind of life he enjoys:

Ohno speaks to a group of elementary students in Arlington, Virginia, about staying away from alcohol and other trouble. He often shares the story of his rebellious teen years in hopes of keeping other young people from making similar mistakes.

> [Speed skating] first allowed me to focus all of my energies on something else positive. It really allowed me to explore who I was and my own talents in my sport. [I] was blessed that the sport helped change my life and that I had a great dad who pushed me into the right direction. A lot of kids, sometimes they don't have parents who support them the way my dad did. That's why I'm so passionate about it, because I feel like I was one of the lucky ones. A lot of kids out there don't have the same scenario out there set up like I did. I just want to kind of allow them and get them to know that anything they do is up to them.

Quoted in Matt Baker. "Up Close: Apolo Anton Ohno." *Tulsa World*, April 20, 2010.

Six days later, Ohno skated in the five-hundred meter and the five-thousand-meter team relay. In a Twitter post that morning Ohno proclaimed, "It's time. Heart of a lion. I will give my all—heart, mind & spirit today. This is what it's about! All the way until the end! No regrets."[91] But another of the freak occurrences that make short track speed skating so volatile caught up with Ohno in the first race. He crossed the finish line in second place behind Charles Hamelin to apparently win a silver medal. But judges soon disqualified Ohno for having impeded Canadian François-Louis Tremblay on the final turn.

Ohno had only a short time to be upset over the ruling because he also had to skate the five-thousand-meter relay with teammates Celski, Simon Cho, Travis Jayner, and Jordan Malone. Skating the vital last few laps, Ohno charged by the Chinese team to give the U.S. squad a third place finish for a bronze medal that pushed Ohno's already historic medal count to eight. Ohno told reporters, "I feel totally happy, totally at peace with what this team accomplished. I couldn't be more satisfied."[92]

It was Ohno's last race of the 2010 Winter Olympics. Reporters also asked if it was his last Olympics. Ohno responded noncommitally by saying, "I never say never. But I need a break from this sport."[93]

"I Have No Fear"

Ohno took a vacation from skating for the rest of 2010. He wrote a second autobiography and pursued business interests, such as creating his own line of nutritional supplements, and acting in the movies and on television. Although many people would be scared to try to start a new career, Ohno was confident he could do whatever he attempted. He said, "Coming from a sports background, whether I want to be on TV or go into the business world. I have no fear."[94]

The Olympic hero also continued to try to be a positive role model for young people. He created the Apolo Anton Ohno Foundation to help young people and has visited many schools to tell students they can accomplish great things if they work

Ohno holds a copy of his second autobiography, titled Zero Regrets, at a booksigning event in October 2010.

hard. In inspirational talks, Ohno explains his life story, including the mistakes he made when he was younger that almost ruined his chances to win an Olympic medal. At Dwight D. Eisenhower Middle School in Laurel, Maryland, he told students, "Live active healthy lifestyles, make positive decisions in your life." He also explained that it is not too late to start living like that now because "Life is like sport, and sport is like life. It's not about how you start, it's about how you finish the race."[95]

Many people in 2010 believed Ohno was still not finished with speed skating. Fellow Olympic hero Shani Davis was one of them. In October he said, "Sooner or later I think he'll want to come back [to skating]."[96] If Ohno does, his Olympic legend will undoubtedly grow even greater.

Notes

Introduction: A Genius on Ice

1. Quoted in Dan Kelly. "Icebreaker." *Boys' Life*, January 1999. p. 12.
2. Quoted in Boxing-Memorabilia.com. "Muhammad Ali Sayings." Boxing-Memorabilia.com. http://www.boxing-memorabilia.com/Muhammad_Ali_Quotes.html.
3. Jae Su Chun. Interview with the author. Pettit National Ice Center, Milwaukee, WI. December 9, 2010.
4. Shani Davis. Interview with the author. Pettit National Ice Center, Milwaukee, WI. December 9, 2010.
5. Apolo Anton Ohno. *Zero Regrets*. New York: Atria, 2010. p. 29.

Chapter 1: A Father and Son Alone

6. Quoted in Ron Claiborne. "Apolo Ohno Has a Single Father Behind His Success." ABCNews.com. June 18, 2006. http://abcnews.go.com/GMA/ESPNSports/story?id=2090015&page=1.
7. Quoted in Elliott Almond. "Winter Olympic Profile Apolo Ohno—Completing a Family Circle." *Seattle Times*, January 15, 1998. http://community.seattletimes.nwsource.com/archive/?date=19980115&slug=2728777.
8. Apolo Anton Ohno with Nancy Ann Richardson. *A Journey: The Autobiography of Apolo Anton Ohno*. New York: Simon & Schuster, 2002. p. 13.
9. Quoted in Ron Corning. "Father's Day." *Good Morning America*, ABC, June 18, 2006.
10. Ohno with Richardson. *A Journey*. p. 16.
11. Quoted in Matt Baker. "Up Close: Apolo Anton Ohno." *Tulsa World*, April 20, 2010.
12. Quoted in Claiborne. "Apolo Ohno Has a Single Father Behind His Success."
13. Quoted in Michele Deppe. "From Green Eggs to Gold Medals." *Highlights for Children*, December 2006. p. 32.

14. Quoted in Lynn Thompson. "Gold-Medal Dad: Yuki Ohno on Raising an Olympic Sensation." *Seattle Times*, June 18, 2002.
15. Quoted in Claiborne. "Apolo Ohno Has a Single Father Behind His Success."
16. Quoted in Denise Henry. "BLAST OFF! Apolo Ohno's Amazing Journey." *Scholastic Scope*, December 13, 2002. p. 18.
17. Ohno. *Zero Regrets*. p. 29.

Chapter 2: Ohno Becomes a Speed Skater

18. Quoted in Percy Allen. "Fed. Way Speedskater Decides to Take His Time." *Seattle Times*, March 15, 1996. http://community.seattletimes.nwsource.com/archive/?date=19960315&slug=2319087.
19. Quoted in Deppe. "From Green Eggs to Gold Medals." p. 32.
20. Apolo Ohno. "Kids Who Are Getting the Most Out of Sports." *Sports Illustrated for Kids*, March 1996. p. 17.
21. Ohno with Richardson. *A Journey*. p. 27.
22. Quoted in Percy Allen. "Fed. Way Speedskater Decides to Take His Time." *Seattle Times*, March 15, 1996. http://community.seattletimes.nwsource.com/archive/?date=19960315&slug=2319087.
23. Patrick Wentland. Telephone interview with the author. November 10, 2010.
24. Quoted in Ron Claiborne. "Apolo's Mother Left When He Was One." ESPN Sports, June 18, 2006. http://abcnews.go.com/GMA/ESPNSports/story?id=2090015&page=1.
25. Quoted in Elliott Almond. "Winter Olympic Profile Apolo Ohno—Completing a Family Circle." *Seattle Times*, January 15, 1998. http://community.seattletimes.nwsource.com/archive/?date=19980115&slug=2728777.
26. Quoted in Claiborne. "Apolo's Mother Left When He Was One."
27. Quoted in S. L. Price. "Launch of Apolo." *Sports Illustrated*, February 4, 2002. p. 122.
28. Quoted in Almond. "Winter Olympic Profile Apolo Ohno."

29. Quoted in Lynn Zinser. "A Long Road to Olympic Short-Track." *(Colorado Springs, CO) Gazette*, December 15, 2001.
30. Ohno. *Zero Regrets*. p. 55.
31. Wentland. Telephone interview with the author.
32. Ohno. *Zero Regrets*. p. 57.
33. Quoted in Kelly. "Icebreaker." p. 12.

Chapter 3: Ohno Decides to Pursue Greatness

34. Quoted in Claiborne. "Apolo's Mother Left When He Was One."
35. Ohno. *Zero Regrets*. p. 71.
36. Quoted in Mike DeArmond. "Ohno Moved Past That Rock and a Hard Place." *Kansas City Star*, February 12, 2002.
37. Quoted in Claiborne. "Apolo's Mother Left When He Was One."
38. Ohno. *Zero Regrets*. p. 83.
39. Quoted in Kelly. "Icebreaker." p. 12.
40. Ohno with Richardson. *A Journey*. p. 77.
41. Ohno. *Zero Regrets*. p. 113.
42. Quoted in Zinser. "A Long Road to Olympic Short-Track."

Chapter 4: The 2002 Winter Olympics

43. Quoted in Meri-Jo Borzilleri. "Ohno's Streak Ends; Davis Becomes First Black Person to Make Speedskating Team." *(Colorado Springs, CO) Gazette*, December 22, 2001.
44. Quoted in Ron C. Judd. "Winter Olympics Notebook: Ohno's Slow Go Won't Die Down." *Seattle Times*, January 20, 2002.
45. Quoted in Borzilleri. "Ohno's Streak Ends; Davis Becomes First Black Person to Make Speedskating Team."
46. Tony Goskowicz. Interview with the author. Pettit National Ice Center, Milwaukee, WI. December 9, 2010.
47. Quoted in DeArmond. "Ohno Moved Past That Rock and a Hard Place."
48. S.L. Price. "Launch of Apolo." *Sports Illustrated*, February 4, 2002. p. 122.

49. Quoted in Lynn Hoppes. "Apolo Ohno So Glad for His Father's Tough Love." ESPN, June 18, 2010. http://espn.go.com/espn/page2/index?id=5301584.
50. Quoted in Price. "Launch of Apolo." p. 122.
51. Quoted in Associated Press. "We Have Liftoff: Ohno Takes Second in 1,000-Meter Heat in Olympic Debut." SI.com, February 13, 2002. http://sportsillustrated.cnn.com/olympics/2002/speed_skating/news/2002/02/13/mens_1000_ap/.
52. Quoted in Liz Robbins. "Ohno Slides to Silver After Wild Collision Near Finish." *New York Times*, February 16, 2002.
53. Quoted in Associated Press. "Ohno Returns to Ice Despite Suffering from Leg Injury." SI.com, February 18, 2002. http://sportsillustrated.cnn.com/olympics/2002/speed_skating/news/2002/02/18/ohno_ap/.
54. Quoted in Associated Press. "Ohno Captures Gold After Winner Disqualified." SI.com, February 20, 2002. http://sportsillustrated.cnn.com/olympics/2002/speed_skating/news/2002/02/20/short_track_ap/.
55. Quoted in Associated Press. "Ohno Comes up Short in Bid to Capture Four Medals." SI.com, February 23, 2002. http://sportsillustrated.cnn.com/olympics/2002/speed_skating/news/2002/02/23/short_track_ap/.

Chapter 5: The 2006 Winter Olympics

56. Quoted in Ron Judd. "Spotlight Beckons Again for Ohno." *Seattle Times*, February 9, 2006. http://seattletimes.nwsource.com/html/olympics/2002792704_olyohno09.html.
57. Ohno with Richardson. *A Journey*. p. 143.
58. Quoted in Brian Cazeneuve. "Apolo Anton Ohno." *Sports Illustrated*, February 13, 2006. p. 45.
59. Quoted in Tony Overman. "Swooners at Capitol Prove Ohno-Mania Still Burns Hot." *Olympian*, March 15, 2002. http://news.theolympian.com/specialsections/Legislature2002/20020315/125442.shtml.

60. Quoted in Brian Cazeneuve. "Still on the Fast Track." *Sports Illustrated*, December 13, 2004. http://sportsillustrated.cnn.com/vault/article/magazine/MAG1114724/index.html.
61. Quoted in Michelle Orecklin. "You Never Know Who You'll Meet." *Time*, June 10, 2002. p. 75.
62. Quoted in Chris Jones. "One Thing Perfectly: Catching Up with Apolo Ohno." *Esquire*, February 1, 2006. http://www.esquire.com/features/the-game/ESQ0206GAME_72.
63. Quoted in Gavin Edwards. "Short-track speed skater Apolo Ohno took off at Salt Lake Games, and he's yet to come down." *Rolling Stone*, March 11, 2002. p. 111.
64. Quoted in Vicki Michaelis. "Ohno Returns with No-Frills Regimen." *USA Today*, February 6, 2003.
65. Quoted in Jones, "One Thing Perfectly: Catching Up with Apolo Ohno."
66. Quoted in John Griffiths. "American Gold." *Teen People*, November 2002. p. 124.
67. Quoted in Brian Cazeneuve. "We Have Liftoff—Again, Apolo Ohno Is Back to Prove His Big '02 Was No Fluke." *Sports Illustrated*, November 1, 2005. http://sportsillustrated.cnn.com/2005/writers/brian_cazeneuve/11/01/ohno/index.html.
68. Quoted in Vicki Michaelis. "Speedskater Ohno Faces Old Ghosts." *USA Today*, September 22, 2005.
69. Quoted in Brian Cazeneuve. "Apolo Still Has His Edge." *Sports Illustrated*, February 22, 2010. p. 44.
70. Quoted in Karen Crouse. "Ohno Is Hoping for Victories and Thaw in Icy Relations with South Koreans." *New York Times*, February 12, 2006.
71. Cazeneuve. "We Have Liftoff."
72. Quoted in Ted Keith. "On the Fast Track." *Sports Illustrated for Kids*, February 2006. p. 34.
73. Quoted in Associated Press. "Ohno Fails in Attempt to Defend 1,500 Gold." NBC Sports, February 27, 2006. http://nbcsports.msnbc.com/id/11281804/.
74. Quoted in Yen Yi-Wyn Yen. "The Wrath of Ahn." *Sports Illustrated*, February 27, 2006. p. 73.

75. Quoted in Karen Crouse. "Ohno Captures Gold and Helps Brighten Games for the U.S." *New York Times*, February 26, 2006. http://www.nytimes.com/2006/02/26/sports/olympics/26short.html?ref=apolo_anton_ohno.
76. Quoted in John Crumpackere. "OHNO—OH YES! No need to Apolo-gize for Gold-Bronze Finish." *San Francisco Chronicle*, February 2, 2006.

Chapter 6: The 2010 Winter Olympics

77. Quoted in Bernie Wilson. "Oh, What a Night." Yahoo! Sports, February 25, 2006. http://sports.yahoo.com/olympics/torino2006/short_track/news?slug=bw-ohno022506&prov=yhoo&type=lgns.
78. Ohno. *Zero Regrets*. p. 198.
79. Quoted in John Gillie. "Sponsorship Deal Comes as Seattle-Area Speed Skater Trains for Olympics in Vancouver, B.C." *Olympian*, November 18, 2009. http://www.theolympian.com/2009/11/18/1040712/ohnos-image-takes-off-with-alaska.html.
80. Quoted in Dean Rutz. "Apolo Ohno of Seattle Dominated at Nationals." *Seattle Times*, February 26, 2007. http://seattletimes.nwsource.com/html/othersports/2003589075_winter26.html.
81. Quoted in *Seattle Times*. "Ohno Captures 8th National Title." *Seattle Times*, February 26, 2007. http://seattletimes.nwsource.com/html/othersports/2003589075_winter26.html.
82. Ohno. *Zero Regrets*. p. 201.
83. Quoted in Monica Rizzo. "Ohno A-Go-Go." *People*, April 30, 2007. http://storage.people.com/jpgs/20070430/20070430-750-87.jpg.
84. Quoted in Jennifer Wulff, Monica Rizzo, and Michelle Tan. "IT'S APOLO!" *People*, June 4, 2007. p. 52.
85. Quoted in Greg Bishop. "Picking Up a Career in Perfect Stride." *New York Times*, March 7, 2009. http://www.nytimes.com/2009/03/08/sports/othersports/08ohno.html?ref=apolo_anton_ohno.

86. Quoted in Greg Bishop. "Up a Mountain, Olympic Dreams Are Carved." *New York Times*, August 2, 2008. http://www.nytimes.com/2008/08/02/sports/olympics/02incline.html?ref=apolo_anton_ohno.
87. Quoted in Vicki Michaelis. "Speedskating Icon Ohno Aims to Dance into 2010 Games." *USA Today*, October 10, 2008. http://www.usatoday.com/sports/olympics/2008-10-22-ohno-2010_N.html.
88. Rebecca Sun. "Six Things to Like." *Sports Illustrated*, February 8, 2010. p. 73.
89. Quoted in Cazeneuve. "Apolo Still Has His Edge." pp. 43–44.
90. Quoted in Greg Bishop. "Ohno Stakes Claim as U.S. King of Winter." *New York Times*, February 21, 2010. http://www.nytimes.com/2010/02/21/sports/olympics/21ohno.html?ref=apolo_anton_ohno.
91. Quoted in Greg Bishop. "Disqualified in 500, Ohno Wins 8th Medal." *New York Times*, February 26, 2010. http://www.nytimes.com/2010/02/27/sports/olympics/27ohno.html?ref=apolo_anton_ohno.
92. Quoted in Phil Taylor. "Record Night Proves to Be just a Snapshot of Ohno's Entire Career." *Sports Illustrated*, February 27, 2010. http://sportsillustrated.cnn.com/2010/olympics/2010/writers/phil_taylor/02/27/ohno.column/.
93. Quoted in Bishop. "Ohno Stakes Claim as U.S. King of Winter."
94. Quoted in Sean Gregory. "Apolo Ohno." *Time*, February 15, 2010. p. 44.
95. Quoted in Lindsey McPherson. "Olympic Skater Brings a Winning Message: Apolo Ohno Is Highlight of Program at Eisenhower Middle." *Laurel (MD) Leader*, April 21, 2010.
96. Shani Davis. Interview with the author. Pettit National Ice Center, Milwaukee, WI. December 9, 2010.

Important Dates

1982
On May 22 Apolo Anton Ohno is born in Federal Way, Washington; before he is one-year-old, his mother, Jerrie Lee, leaves the family, and his parents divorce.

1994
In February, Ohno watches the Winter Olympics held in Lillehammer, Norway, and becomes interested in short track speed skating; in March, he skates on ice for the first time.

1996
In January, thirteen-year-old Ohno competes in the U.S. Junior World Speed Skating Championships and finishes fourth; in the spring, Ohno is invited to join the U.S. junior national team and train in Lake Placid, New York; on July 8, Ohno flies to Lake Placid to begin training as a short track speed skater.

1997
In March, Ohno wins the U.S. National Short Track Speed Skating Championships at age fourteen to become the youngest national champion ever in his sport; in December he fails to make the U.S. team for the 1998 Winter Olympics.

1998
In January, Ohno spends time alone at a resort in Copalis Beach, Washington, and decides he wants to continue to skate; in March, he wins the final spot on the senior World Cup team; in November, the sixteen-year-old Ohno becomes the youngest skater to win a World Cup race.

1999

In January, Ohno becomes the first U.S. skater to win the overall title at the U.S. Junior Speedskating World Championships in Montreal, Canada.

2002

In February, Ohno wins a gold and a silver medal at the 2002 Winter Olympics in Salt Lake City, Utah.

2005

In October, Ohno competes in South Korea for the first time since 2002 when he made South Koreans angry by winning a gold medal at the expense of a skater from that country.

2006

In February, Ohno wins three more medals—one gold and two bronze—at the 2006 Winter Olympics in Turin, Italy.

2007

On May 22, Ohno and partner Julianne Hough win the *Dancing with the Stars* competition.

2010

In February, Ohno wins three more medals—one silver and two bronze—at the 2010 Winter Olympics in Vancouver, British Columbia, Canada, to boost his career medal count to eight, more than any U.S. Winter Olympian ever.

For More Information

Books

Rebecca Aldridge, *Asian Americans of Achievement: Apolo Anton Ohno*. New York: Chelsea House, 2009. This biography competently explains Ohno's life.

Apolo Anton Ohno with Nancy Ann Richardson. *A Journey: The Autobiography of Apolo Anton Ohno*. New York: Simon & Schuster, 2002. This is Ohno's first autobiography, written after the 2002 Winter Olympics.

Apolo Anton Ohno. *Zero Regrets*. New York: Atria, 2010. Ohno wrote this, his second autobiography, following the 2010 Winter Olympics.

Periodicals

Greg Bishop. "Ohno Stakes Claim as U.S. King of Winter." *New York Times*, February 21, 2010.

Michele Deppe. "From Green Eggs to Gold Medals." *Highlights for Children*, December 2006. This article discusses how Ohno turned himself into an Olympic champion.

Dan Kelly. "Icebreaker." *Boys' Life*, January 1999. This article highlights Ohno's youth and early skating career.

S.L. Price. "Launch of Apolo." *Sports Illustrated*, February 4, 2002. This article provides a fine biographical sketch of Ohno's early skating career.

Websites

Apolo Anton Ohno (http://www.apoloantonohno.com). Ohno's official website offers stories, pictures, and other information about the Olympic champion.

Apolo and Julianne Fansite (http://www.apolojulianne.com/). This site is devoted to Ohno and Hough's 2007 victory in the *Dancing with the Stars* television show.

GotApolo.com (http://www.gotapolo.com/). This fan site is a source of news, information, and pictures about Apolo Anton Ohno.

Internet Movie Database (http://www.imdb.com). This site provides information on movies and television shows, including Apolo Anton Ohno's television appearances, interviews, pictures, and links to more information about him.

TheOfficialPageOf.com (http://theofficialpageof.com). This site offers information on celebrities, including Apolo Anton Ohno.

US Speedskating (http://www.usspeedskating.org/). This is the official website for the U.S. national speed skating team. It includes a biography of Apolo Anton Ohno.

Index

A
Ahn Hyun-Soo, 54, 70, 73
Ali, Muhammad, 10
Apolo Anton Ohno Foundation, 85, 87
Autobiography, 85, *86*

B
Baver, Allison, 75–76
Booksigning event, *86*
Bradbury, Steve, 54, *55*

C
Celebrity status. *See* Fame
Celski, J.R., 82
Charity work, 84, *84*, 85, 87
Childhood
 bicycle riding, 18
 first attempts at speed skating, 24
 heroes, 10
 initial interest in speed skating, 23
 invitation to train in Lake Placid, 28–29
 junior team training, 25, 28–32
 personality, 19–20
 swimming and inline skating, 22–23
Chun, Jae Su, 10–11, 81
Clinton, Bill, 63
Competitive spirit, 12
Controversy, 48–50, 66

Copalis Beach, Washington, 36–38
Creswell, Dave, 40

D
Dancing with the Stars (television show), 75–80, *78*
Dating, 75–76
Davis, Shani, 11–12, 27, *27*, 48–50, *49*, 87
Diet, 69, 81

E
Endorsements, 75

F
Fame, 61–63, 74–75, 80
Fans, 58, 62
Fathers of athletes, 19
 See also Ohno, Yuki
Friends, 27
Future in skating, 87

G
Gagnon, Marc, 54
Gold medals, Olympic, 57, 59, *59*
Greek language, 8

H
Hedrick, Chad, 21, *21*
Heiden, Eric, 51
Heroes, 10
Hough, Julianne, 77–80, *78*

I
Injuries, 43–44
Inline skating, 22
ISU World Short Track Speed Skating Championships, 43, 44, 77

J
Jang, Jimmy, 81
Jansen, Dan, 24
Japan, 34–35, *40*
Junior national team, 25, 28–32, 39
Junior Speedskating World Championships, 42–43

K
Kim Dong-Sung, 42, 54, 57
Korea, South, 66–69, *67*

L
Lake Placid, New York, 25, 28–32, 39
Lee Ho Suk, 70
Leno, Jay, 61–62, *63*
Li Jiajun, 54
Li Ye, *70*
Lifestyle, 65–26, 74
Locke, Gary, 62

M
Manning, Archie, 19
Martial arts, 70
Medals, Olympic, record number of, 82, 83, 85
Media, 50–51

Mental training, 40
Monroe, John, 28
Mother, 14–16

N
Nagano Olympics. *See* Olympics, 1998
Name, 8–10

O
O'Hare, Tommy, 48–50
Ohno, Yuki, *18, 20*
  Apolo's decision concerning his future, 36–38
  being an athletes' father, 19
  immigration to America, 14–15
  rift with son, 29–30
  single fatherhood, 13, 15–18
  strictness, 20, 22
  support of training, 26–28
  videotaping son's performance, *26*
Olympic medals, record number of, 82, *83*, 85
Olympic speed skating athletes, 21
Olympics, 1994, 23
Olympics, 1998, 34–35, *40*
Olympics, 2002, *45*, *53*
  controversy, 48–50, 66
  fans, 52–54, 58
  fifteen-hundred-meter race, 57, 59, *59*
  medal totals, 59–60
  media predictions, 50–51
  qualifying trials, 46–47, 49

100 Apolo Anton Ohno

thousand-meter race,
  54–57, *55*
U.S. skating team, *47*
Olympics, 2006, *31*, 69–73,
  70, *72*
Olympics, 2010, 82, *83*, 85
Otter, Jeroen, 34

P
Personality
  childhood, 19–20
  competitive spirit, 12
  sportsmanship, 56–57
  teenage rebelliousness, 22

S
Safety equipment, 41, *41*
Salt Lake City Olympics. *See*
  Olympics, 2002
Seattle, Washington, *15*
Shimabukuro, Ryan, 21
Smith, Rusty, *49*, 59
South Korea, 66–69, *67*
Speed skating
  Apolo's decision concerning
    his future, 36–38
  equipment, 41, *41*
  first attempts, 24
  future in, 87
  initial interest in, 23
  ISU World Short Track Speed
    Skating Championships,
    43, *44*
  junior national team, 25,
    28–32, 39
  Junior Speedskating World
    Championships, 42–43

short track events, 25, 52
tactics, 64
talent, 10–12
U.S. Short Track
  Championships, 32–34, 64,
  64, 77
World Cup events, 39, 42,
  43–44, 81–82
See also Olympics
Sports psychology, 40

T
Tactics, race, 64
Talent, 10–12
Teenagers, helping, 84, *84*,
  85, 87
Television, 75–76
Television appearances,
  61–62
The Tonight Show with Jay Leno
  (television show), 61–62, *63*
Training
  for 2010 Olympics, 81–82
  diet and exercise, 69–70
  junior national team, 25,
    30–32, 39
  preparation for the 2006
    Olympics, 65
  U.S. Olympic Complex,
    Colorado Springs,
    Colorado, 32
  workout schedule, 79
Tremblay, Francois-Louis,
  71–73
Turcotte, Mathieu, 54
Turin Olympics. *See* Olympics,
  2006

U
U.S. Olympic Complex,
 Colorado Springs, Colorado,
 32, 65
U.S. Short Track Championships,
 32–34, 64, 64, 77

W
W magazine, 63
Wentland, Patrick, 28, 30–32,
 39–40, 42

White Ring Stadium, *34*
Williams, Richard, 19
Woods, Earl, 19
Workout schedule. *See* Training
World Cup events, 39, 42–44,
 81–82

Picture Credits

Cover Photo: Frederick M. Brown/Getty Images
© Andre Jenny/Alamy, 32
AP Images/Amy Sancetta, 23, 31, 70
AP Images/Anna Mia Davidson, 18
AP Images/Douglas C. Pizac, 26, 47, 49
AP Images/Elaine Thompson, 75
AP Images/Kevork Djansezian, 41, 72
AP Images/Laurent Rebours, 44
AP Images/Lionel Cironneau, 59
AP Images/Matt Dunham, 21
AP Images/Yun Jai-hyoung, 67
Boris Streubel/Bongarts/Getty Images, 27
© Christopher Morris/Corbis, 12
David Gray/Reuters/Landov, 55
© Duomo/Corbis, 40
Ezra Shaw/Getty Images, 53
George Rose/Getty Images, 15
Jamie Squire/Getty Images, 58, 64, 83
Jason Merritt/FilmMagic/Getty Images, 78
Kris Connor/Getty Images, 84
Margaret Norton/NBC/Getty Images, 63
Mike Powell/Allsport/Getty Images, 34
Robert Laberge/Getty Images, 45
Scott Halleran/Podium AAO/Getty Images, 10
Statia Photography/Getty Images, 20
Steve Mack/FilmMagic/Getty Images, 86

About the Author

Michael V. Uschan is the author of eighty-one books, including *Life of An American Soldier in Iraq*, for which he won the 2005 Council for Wisconsin Writers Juvenile Nonfiction Award. Uschan began his career as a writer and editor with United Press International, a wire service that provided stories to newspapers, radio, and television. Uschan considers writing history books a natural extension of the skills he developed in his many years as a journalist. He and his wife, Barbara, reside in the Milwaukee suburb of Franklin, Wisconsin.